AF487350

A Feast of Flames

Brent Perry

This book is dedicated to not just one person or thing. I will always thank my children for giving me the light that I have in my life. They are my world. I also would like to say that this book is dedicated to anyone who has ever felt so bogged down and destitute in their lives in any way, but somehow has found a way to pick themselves up and just soldier on. Keep moving forward, this book is for you… for us!

Chapters

CHAPTER 1
BLOOD DRAWN

The slapping echoes of our boots and shoes colliding with the stone floor reverberated down the corridor, practically screaming out our location to everyone and everything in the building. This abandoned hospital turned Order of Saint Patrick stronghold radiated an aura of malevolence to any who dared trespass in its inner workings. Yet, the Order had been too empty-headed to see the spirits that still roamed these halls, let alone feel the grudge that had seeped in and stained these now unconsecrated grounds.

One would assume that these supposed men of God would sense so much negative energy and literal evil that bled from the very cement that the building was made of. But no, their blind faith numbed their senses and dulled that natural instinct that most humans have that tells them to get out of dangerous places and situations. Sure, their faith somehow protected them from most of the mundane supernatural entities. But not all of the supernatural, and clearly not what was present here.

Thanks to Vergil's contacts in the Order of Saint Patrick, we had learned of this location as a possible detainment facility for prisoners of the Order. Unfortunately, the building's exact location was irritatingly more complicated to locate. This had caused me to think that we had missed our target altogether. But that wasn't the case here. It wasn't as if Vergil's information and coordinates were bad. Hell, we were able to Google search the building's location and get a decent amount of information about the place. We learned that the building had once been a hospital for mentally ill patients and had been shut down due to deplorable living conditions and abuse of the patients from the staff. Or, that was the official story. Apparently, the truth was that the patients revolted one day and murdered a large portion of the staff on duty. The place was shut down almost immediately after that and no one knows what had happened to the remaining patients. To this day, most people agreed that the whole property was haunted.

And therein lied the problem… the place was most definitely haunted. So much in fact that the spectral denizens that dwelled there managed to render it completely unperceivable to average people.

Sadly, this had not been the case with the Order of Saint Patrick. They had blundered in after discovering and probably purchasing the property and had stirred up the souls condemned to dwell within by renovating the entire building and transforming it into a fortress.

In the end, their faith had not been enough to protect them from what they disturbed. The very foundations that the building had been built on seemed to have awoken, and it was pretty pissed off. One by one, the Brethren of the Order that had resided within their new stronghold had been driven mad. The spirits had whittled down and had overcome any and all vestments of protection that their faith had once provided them. Now, most were apparently helpless, insane, and tortured by the very patients that had once suffered in this building while they were alive.

Some of the Brethren wandered the halls, continuing to perform the everyday tasks on an endless cycle of repentance. Tasks such as reporting to the main headquarters of the Order of Saint Patrick that everything was normal; or, bringing the supplied deliveries inside to keep up appearances. These drones were few, unable to break away from whatever force compelled them to perform their actions in an endless loop.

And then there were the even rarer individuals whose madness had driven them to violent frenzies. Well, at least they had become violent upon seeing Rook, Vergil, and me wandering the labyrinthal halls of the building. We had been prepared to fight the Order, but we were woefully ill equipped to deal with what we encountered. Aside from the mad Brothers of the Order, there were also the wandering poltergeists manifesting and attacking our ragtag trio. Some were head-on charging us in direct attacks. Most used some form of psycho-kinesis to throw dangerous projectiles at us, or just throw us.

"Gee, it would be real nice to have the Arch Angel who has magical powers and control of the dead here with us now!" Rook shouted as a pair of scissors and a stapler embedded themselves into the wall by our heads. We twisted around a corner, taking cover from any more random missiles.

"Yeah, well he was worried that the Order might have laid a trap for us and didn't want to risk becoming enslaved to them since they have Eve under their thumb." I replied, breaking open my shotgun to eject the empty shells.

"Can't say that it was a bad idea." Rook grumbled. "But it would still be nice to have a heavy hitter on our side right now."

I nodded in silent agreement as I loaded two rock-salt shells and flicked the breach of my gun closed. I leaned my body mere inches around the corner to try and gain a visual of our spectral assailant. And as my eye poked just enough past the edge of the wall, I found myself locking sight with the yellow and black iris of the poltergeist. I lost my balance and staggered backwards, but not before the ghost had shouted "BOO!" In retrospect, it would have been hilarious had our lives not been on the line.

In my flailing and failing attempt to distance myself from the ghost, I found myself flat on my ass and scrambling to get my bearings. My gun went skidding across the floor as a sudden weight materialized on my chest and shoulders. The bodily form of the poltergeist with the yellow eyes sat atop my, pinning me down.. In life, it had clearly been a well built orderly or nurse of some sort. Now it was a construct of ectoplasm based on the imprinted memory of the shade straddled over my prone body. Its skin was garishly white, monochromatically void of any signs or colors of life.

A ghastly cackle erupted from his malicious grin as he reached his hand out toward the wall that I had just been leaning against. The imbedded scissors pulled free and rocketed through the air, straight into the ghost's outstretched hand. In a display of inhuman speed the poltergeist buried the dual blades into my shoulder before I had a chance to even take a breath or blink. A scream of distressed pain escaped my lips, followed by the blades being yanked free. My blood spattered across my face and the floor as the spirit held the sheers dauntingly above my head. I could hear guns firing off somewhere in the background, but I couldn't tell who was shooting.

"Any… last… words?!" the poltergeist croaked as he shifted his weight from my unwounded shoulder to my arm, exposing a new target.

I became distantly aware that while the accursed ghost was taunting me, my fingers had begun to draw circular patterns in my blood on the floor. But I could not focus on it any further, as the scissors were slammed through their intended target of my unwounded shoulder. My teeth ached from the sounds of the metal of the blades scraping against the cement floor beneath me.

Through the pain, all but a part of me in the back of my mind gave up. I let a cool flush of calmness wash over me as I accepted my fate and resigned to die. Apparently, that same, small part of me was at odds with the rest of me; as I felt my hand struggle through the pain and grab the scissors over the poltergeist's hand. I forced the blades down and held both of them firmly in place.

A look of confusion replaced the specter's malice as he tried to figure out what I was doing. I watched his physical body begin to fetter and lose its corporeal connection for the briefest of moments. He began to struggle against my grip, pulling frantically to free himself. He pulled one final time and I released my grasp, sending his deteriorating body spilling backwards. Before the ghost could remember that he could vanish and disappear, I slapped my hand down onto the bloody designs that I had created on the floor beside me. I flailed my other arm, flicking spatters of my blood onto the ectoplasmic face of my would-be dispatcher.

"FERRUM VITAE EXSILIO!" I shouted.

I felt the blood beneath my palm heat up as a fiery light encircled the poltergeist and me. The circle flared brighter and brighter, intensely flashing as the ghost exploded into smoldering cinders.

I immediately felt exhausted and let my head fall to rest on the cold floor as the particles of ectoplasm burned to ash, dancing in the air above me. I could only hope that the adrenaline from this near death experience would last long enough for me to pull the scissors out of my shoulder. I groaned at the thought and sat up slowly. Everything seemed foggy and out of focus. I wasn't even aware that Vergil and Rook were kneeling down next to me until Rook spoke up and broke the silence.

"Danny, are you alright?!" Rook boomed.

"Aside from just getting stabbed by a ghost who takes arts and crafts way too seriously, I'm just dandy." I growled.

"Speaking of art, what did you do just now?" Vergil asked, turning his attention to the blood on the floor beside me. "This is clearly the alchemical magic of Solomon. But which spell did you specifically perform?"

I looked to my side and saw an intricate but sloppily drawn transmutation seal painted on the floor. I knew for a fact that I had never seen it before, yet I knew without a doubt which seal it was and what I had performed.

"I transmuted the iron in my blood and used it to sever the anchor that tethered the poltergeist to this realm of existence." I answered mechanically.

"You can do that?" Rook asked.

"I can now, apparently." I answered. "But the real questions we should ask, are 'how' and 'why?'"

"That will have to be a mystery for another time." Vergil interrupted. "We are here to check on the female prisoner that was reported to be incarcerated at this facility. And now we face another obstacle. Danyael, you are now officially the proverbial monkey wrench in the cogs of the original plan."

"You know just what to say to make a man feel special." I replied snidely.

"He's right." Rook added. "You're going to have to let us take the lead from here on out. I know that's not your style, but unless you can do more of those fireworks with your blood… you're just going to wind up getting in our way in your condition."

"I'm fine!" I lied as I yanked the scissors out of my shoulder.

I struggled to keep the agonizing pain from showing on my face, but it didn't last. After a moment of anticipatory silence, I screamed out every swear word I knew in every language that I could speak. I knew that both of them were watching me with their judgmental looks of disapproval. I had become used to it here of late and knew it well. But in this moment I refused to give them the knowledge that I had seen. Slowly and shakily, I rose to my feet, hoping that I wouldn't collapse from the nausea that was washing over me from the pain. I walked over to my gun and picked it up. Even with its small, sawed-off size, its weight pained me to grasp it in a closed hand. I gritted my teeth and clenched it tightly as I slowly drug its heft through the air and dropped it into its holster.

"Fine!" I spat with my back still turned to them. "But let's get out of this area before any more murder spooks come to call!"

Rook grunted his agreement and returned to the hallway that we had been in before we were attacked. Vergil nodded at me to follow silently. I answered with a well timed, seething scowl. Vergil rolled his eyes and continued after Rook.

I took one final glance at the Solomnic transmutation circle drawn in my blood, taking in the memory of what I had just managed to pull off. It felt distant, like a passing thought. I let it leave and returned my focus to our task. I trailed after my friends, leaving the memory just another stain to linger in this dungeon.

CHAPTER 2
A MEETING OF THE MINDS

"We have to stop!" I gasped as I fell against the wall closest to me. "I'm having trouble keeping up and I can't seem to focus."

"In hindsight, we probably should have bandaged his wounds." Vergil commented to Rook.

"YOU THINK?!" I snarled. "Now help me find something that I can use as bandages. I don't think that superglue is going to cut it this time."

"Is that how you have been field treating your wounds?!" Vergil asked, clearly appalled. "It is no small miracle that you have survived as long as you have. Stephen, did you know of this?"

"He has already received the same lecture from me a while ago." Rook answered with a sigh. "I told him that he will regret it in the long run, but he didn't listen to me. And I doubt very seriously he will listen to you. He still is coming to terms with you hanging around more often."

"You both know that I am still right here bleeding all over this wall?!" I interrupted. "Do you think that there would be something around here to patch me up?"

"Given how often that I now know that you get injured," Vergil responded, "I would assume that you would have learned your lesson and would have started to carry at least a remedial first-aid kit with you."

"Less lecturing, more searching!"I ordered bitterly.

I closed my eyes in a futile attempt to keep my head from spinning. I could feel exhaustion creeping throughout my limbs and appendages, making them feel heavier and threatening to infect my mind. I could faintly feel my blood warmly trailing down my arms to my fingertips. The sounds of the world around me became a muffled background noise, almost non-existent. In my growing stupor, I let it all fade into the fog infecting my consciousness. A single drop of blood fell from my index finger into a small puddle that had began to form below my hand in my stillness. The resonance of that solitary drop splashing into the pool of my venous fluids roared like an ocean crashing against the shore in the silence that had blanketed my senses.

Stillness settled on my body; unnatural and comfortable. Everything faded into nothingness, save the sound of my blood occasionally dripping like a cliché water drop into a large, open pool. Was I dying? Was this the final act for me, my curtain call? Would I finally find my peace?

"Hello…" A frail and hoarse voice whispered slowly across the void. "Is someone there?"

"Um… yeah, I think." I answered. "Who are you? Where are you? Where are we? What is this? I thought I was finally dying!"

"You are very close to death." The voice answered weakly. "As am I. The infernal spirits here have kept me alive, but just barely, as I struggle in a state of near death constantly. They delight in watching me suffer."

"Wait, you are in this building?!" I asked fervently. "Are you Eve?!"

"No, my name is Dawn." The voice answered quietly. "I have been a prisoner of the Order and have been here ever since they established this building as a prison and a base of operations."

"Do you know if there are any other prisoners here?" I asked.

"None that have survived." Dawn replied. "But if it is of any help, there has not been a new prisoner here in a very long time."

"Ok, thank you." I said as I came to the realization that the trip here was officially a waste of time. No, I wouldn't think that way. I forced myself to focus. "Where are you being held?"

"Most of the long-term holding cells such as mine are in the basement level." Dawn answered. "That is where I am being held."

"Ok, one last question." I added. "How are we even talking? What is this connection?"

"It is clear to me that we both are beings touched by magic." Dawn stated. "Being so close to death and in such close proximity to one another, I can only guess. It might be that our consciousnesses have drifted through the ambient æther everywhere. I think that it's because of the many breaches in the Veil caused by the mass of spirits pulling energy through to continue haunting this place."

"That sounds way too complicated to be wrong." I replied. "I will need to call Azrael and have him put a stop to the ghastly inhabitants here."

"Wait!" Dawn's voice demanded, hinting the first sign of emotion that I could recall since this connection began. "I need to warn you of what waits down here in the basement level!"

"If you are going to tell me about the murder ghosts, don't." I huffed. "We already know about them. It's actually why I'm in this boat ride of near death."

"No, this is something much worse!" Dawn warned. "One of the Brethren of the Order that patrolled the lower levels was driven mad by the undead souls that dwell here. Over time he… well he did terrible things to many of the other guards of the Order that wandered down here. And when he was done, he ate their remains. He transformed into something monstrous. Something my elders spoke of only in hushed whispers and legends. The only reason that I have survived him is because the spirits do not allow him to harm me. They reserve that torture for themselves."

"Shit…" I managed to mumble as my memory told me what was down in the basement with Dawn.

"Please… do not die!" Dawn pleaded. "I am begging you. Do not destroy this small glimmer of hope that you have given me. Live… an...d... don...t... d..."

`   My eyes snapped open as a surge of pain raced through every fiber of my body. I screamed in agony and sat up immediately in a panic. Wires were connected to adhesive modules stuck to my chest. I looked around in confusion, patting my chest down absently as I attempted to take in my surroundings. My shoulders hurt more than the rest of me. I felt strips of gauze beneath my touch as I brushed my fingers over their opposite shoulders. My eyes followed the cords from my chest and found that they were connected to a portable A. E. D. unit. I looked up from the A. E. D. straight into Vergil's concerned face. Next to him was Rook with a look somewhere between worried concern and seething anger. On the floor between the three of us were the contents of a high-end first-aid kit. Apparently the Order of Saint Patrick spared no expense when it came to the well being of their zealots.

"Danyael," Vergil began slowly, "are you ok? Are you with us?"

"I am now." I groaned as I began ripping the defibrillator pads from my chest. "Where did you find a first-aid kit, let alone an A. E. D. unit?"

"Believe it or not, the Order makes sure that every facility is well equipped with both." Vergil answered. "Standard protocol is to have at least three of each per floor. It was just a matter of locating where they were."

"What about the ghosts with the stab attitudes?" I asked.

"Actually, they have given us a pretty wide berth since you did your finger-painting lightshow." Rook answered. "Although, we did have to knock out a few of emerald pajama-wearing loonies while we were out looking. But that's it."

"Good to know." I said.

"And now that you are patched up and alive and well, we can continue our search for Eve." Vergil announced as he stood up.

"Hold your horses there, buckaroo." I groaned as I followed him to my feet. "She isn't here."

"How can you possibly know that?!" Rook blurted as his larger bulk came level with ours.

"While I was dead, or rather near death, I had… well I'm not sure what to call it." I explained. "Essentially, because of all the ghosts wanting to be ass-holes, they have ripped the Veil here to tethers. Because of that, I was able to talk to a different prisoner here who was also near death. She gave me the rundown of this joint. This leads me to the even bigger problem that we now have."

"What problem?" Rook asked irritably. "I hate bigger problems when it comes to magic and the supernatural."

"Well, you are definitely going to hate this." I replied. "The holding cells for the long term prisoners are in the basement level and apparently there is a wendigo down there."

"A what?!" Rook snapped followed by a low snarl escaped Vergil's mouth behind him as a look of disgust and rage swept across our former enemy's expression. "What the hell is a wendigo?"

"A wendigo is created when a human eats the flesh of another human and their angry spirits curse the one who has imbibed their flesh." Vergil answered bitterly.

"That's what the storybooks and legends would have you believe, and they're not too far off from the truth." I corrected. "It only takes the presence of malevolent spirits while eating humans or eating human flesh on bloodstained or unconsecrated ground. And this place is like the Las Vegas Strip of those categories."

"But the only people who were here were those from the Order… oh crap." Rook trailed as he connected the dots. He placed a hand on Vergil's shoulder awkwardly. "I'm sorry… I know what it's…"

"Thank you Stephen."Vergil whispered harshly.

"Wait a sec!" Rook blurted suddenly. "How do we know that we can even trust this prisoner? Do you even know her name? How do we know she isn't some spook setting a trap for us?"

"She said that her name is Dawn." I answered. "And even if it is a trap, we cannot take the chance of leaving a wendigo unchecked so close to a major city. They really are the stuff of nightmares, Rook. On average, they're about seven feet tall, have long claws on creepily long arms, and they recreationally eat people. They are cursed to always hunger. So they never stop. Usually we don't get them down this far from mountains, but given what this building is; I'm only surprised they haven't let the wendigo out sooner. Come on Vergil, you're better with the words that Rook likes to hear, back me up."

"So, the infamous elfling, Dawn." Vergil murmured absently to himself. "So this is where they kept her."

"Wait, an elf?!" Rook and I asked together.

"Yes, an elf…" Vergil answered astutely, finally returning to the conversation.

"Are we talking about an elf as in Santa's elves," I asked incredulously, "or is she closer to Lord of the Rings elves?"

"If you must use a pop-culture reference to identify her, then I would think Lord of the Rings elves." Vergil sighed.

"First off, Lord of the Rings is not pop-culture." I warned irately. "The books were a phenomenal sensation long before the movies made it culturally cinematic. Secondly, what do you know about Dawn the elf?"

"She is one of the last of her kind." Vergil replied. "She was captured by the Order about a year before you came onto their radar, Danyael. They kept her alive to try to learn where other elves were located so that the Order could deal with them. But given that she was orphaned on a Native-American reservation, it was a futile endeavor."

"You know Vergil; sometimes you open your mouth and the stupid that rolls from your voice makes me want to shoot you in the face." I snapped. "Let me correct your disgusting statement. The Order of Saint Patrick kidnapped this poor girl and tortured her for years in a horrible attempt to get information from her that she did not have so that they could commit genocide, and then they left her to rot in this hell oblivious and uncaring of the fact that the place was swarming with evil spirits. See… I fixed your explanation. See to it that you don't forget that you're not in the Order anymore. Lose their way of speaking or don't speak at all!"

"Forgive me for my absent minded wording." Vergil abashed. "Years of speaking in a certain manner will not be an easy feat to leave behind. But I will redouble my efforts."

"Good…" I growled.

"So… we're going to attempt to rescue this elf and slay the monster?" Rook asked, clearly trying to change the subject and alter the tension.

"That's the gist of it in a nutshell… more or less." I answered in mock-cheer.

"Great, we get to be heroes for a change." Rook chuckled.

"Yup, big damn heroes, sir!" I quoted from Firefly.

"Ain't we just?!" Rook added with a grin. I was happy that he had begun to pick up my geek and nerd reference habits.

"Is it possible for either of you to go a whole twenty-four hours without spouting immature prattle and banter from books, movies, or television?"

"Sorry bub," I replied, patting his back sympathetically, "ain't going to happen."

I stepped past Vergil to lead on, but then I had to backtrack when realized that had no idea where I was going or how to get to the basement. A good-natured chortle still rumbled from Rook as he watched Vergil fume. I leaned down, making sure that Vergil was paying attention to me.

"Yes Danyael?" Vergil growled.

"Yeah, so… I realized that I'm lost. Do either of you know where anything is in this place?" I asked innocently. "I mean, since you both had to search for the first-aid kits, I figured… well, you know…"

"I do know," Rook laughed as I dodged Vergil's hand attempting to swat at my head in irritancy. "I also know where the elevator is. Why don't we just take that?"

"That's a negative." I replied, moving my injured form just out of Vergil's reach. "Technology and the supernatural just don't cooperate under the best of circumstances. I don't want to drop to my death in a small metal box in a building full of supernatural entities that all want to see us die."

"You make a valid point." Rook replied. "Stairs it is then."

"Lead the way Agent Hightower." Vergil added, clearly not wanting to hear me speak again.

And thus began our second trek through the building. This time we moved at a comfortable pace. Thankfully, it didn't take long to find the stairs. They had been built into the North corner of the building. Rook glared resentfully at the winding steps on the other side of the door with pure disdain, and I knew why. He was a smoker and a bit more… well more in his middle region than Vergil or me. This meant difficulties for him if we had to escape up them in a hurry.

"Hey Rook," I said, breaking up his menacing stare down, "Do you have your lighter on you?"

"Yeah, why?" Rook answered.

"Because fire is a wendigo's only known weakness." I replied. "I don't want to get down there and not be prepared."

"That's a great idea," Rook added, "But what fuel are we going to use to burn? I hope that you're not going to try to get close enough to this thing so that you can put the flame directly against it? Because that sounds idiotic and suicidal."

"Oh balls, you're right!" I hissed. "Crap!"

"I guess that it's lucky for both of you that I kept my head where it was needed back there." Vergil interjected as he held out his hand between us. Resting in his palm was a small bottle of rubbing alcohol from the first-aid kit. "You are welcome."

"Yeah, yeah… don't gloat." I chided. "Now Rook, give me your lighter."

"Nope." Rook replied. "We told you earlier that you're benched. That rule still applies. I think that Vergil and I can manage this. Set the giant, man-eating monster on fire before it kills and eats us, right?"

"Well anything sounds easy when you say it like that." I grumbled. "But wendigos are…"

"… Inhumanly fast and unearthly strong." Vergil interrupted. "Danyael, you are not the only person present who has fought a wendigo before and lived to tell the tale."

"Technically I have dispatched a total of three." I corrected. "Four if you count that pale ogre that was mistaken for a wendigo in Yosemite last year. My point is that I nearly died every time, this won't be a cake walk for anyone."

"Awe, see, he does care about us." Rook teased.

"What do you suggest we do then?" Vergil asked, ignoring Rook.

"Call Azrael in as backup." I answered quickly. "He can come and help us now that we know that this is not a trap set by the Order."

"That's not actually a bad idea." Rook agreed.

"Ugh… you are correct. Lord Azrael would be a great help here. Make the call." Vergil sighed.

I nodded grimly and pulled my phone out. I dialed the number of the burner that I had left with the arch angel. I smiled knowing that most people couldn't say that they had the Angel of Death on speed dial. I could. But then again, the Devil had my number as well. That fact I wasn't too keen to brag about. Not because I am religious or anything; mainly because I owed him a favor. Or at least I felt that I did. Lucifer had been mum's the word if he agreed with me or not. Which made the very thought frightening. The phone rang absently four times before I heard the sounds of the line connecting.

"Danyael, am I correct to assume that you need my direct intervention and involvement?" Azrael's voice inquired blankly.

"You would be right." I answered. "Do you need directions here or can you use your angel magic to figure it out?"

"Again, Danyael, it is not angel magic." Azrael lectured. "It is divine power bestowed to me through my Father, the One True…"

"The one true big cheese, yadda, yadda, yadda…" I interrupted. "So you've told me so many times before. Please just answer the question."

"Yes, I can figure it out." Azrael's voice boomed behind me. "Do you know that at the height of my Father's power, mortals were smote for not bowing in reverence to our presence, let alone to give us such cheek as you have so disrespectfully done with me?"

"Yes, well times have changed." I answered as I attempted to usher my heart back down from my throat to my chest. "Besides, you know that I have the upmost respect for you, right? Thanks for coming."

"You are welcome." Azrael laughed. "This whole plot of land reeks of the dead and vile energy. What is going on here?"

So I spent the next few minutes explaining to Azrael everything that had happened from the time we entered the building, what we had learned, and everything that had transpired up until my phone call. His expression never changed from stoic emptiness. He nodded occasionally as I unfurled the details, never stopping me until I had finally caught him up.

"I am afraid that I cannot help you with the wendigo." Azrael announced flatly.

"What?!" Vergil, Rook, and I shouted in near unison.

"Why not?" I snapped.

"A wendigo is still a mortal creature with a human soul. Azrael explained. "Not dead, but neither alive, yet still human. I am bound by Father's law."

"Damn!" I shouted. "I hate his dogmatic laws!"

"I did not say that I would not help you, though." Azrael added. "I can and will do something about these malignant spirits. They have been left unchecked for too long and have caused too much harm to the living and the Veil. I will repair the excess damage that they have inflicted by pulling so much æther through. I only wish that I was capable of cleansing the land of the grudge that has cursed it. Only fire can undo that stain now."

"Fine, do what you can." I said. "We will take care of the rest."

"I suggest that three of you advert your eyes." Azrael warned as he began shrugging off his pea-coat.

We turned away from Azrael and entered through the door to the stairwell. A blinding light filled the small glass window, but none of us turned to watch it. We had our job and knew that the arch angel was more than enough to handle the ghosts that haunted this building. I just hoped that we would be enough to defeat the wendigo and free the poor girl who had been stuck in this hell suffering for Gods only knew how long.

I made a vow to any of them that was listening that tonight would be Dawn's last night as a prisoner and the last night this building would stand. I felt a fire rage in my core as the three of us transcended closer to Hell than I had ever been."

"Shiny, let's be good guys!" I whispered.

CHAPTER 3
ILLUMINATED DANGER

Every step that the three of us took down the empty stairwell echoed so loudly that it sounded like a herd of bison stampeding the descent into the basement. The stairs themselves seemed to be trying to sabotage our efforts of stealth. If it wasn't loose debris getting kicked up and bouncing off of the metal base-plates running the lengths of the walls, it was the noise from our boots hitting the floor and exploding with noise like lightning and thunder booming down into the depths of the empty walk below.

And one would expect the stairway of an evil, haunted building to be poorly lit and riddled with death traps. Nope, not this one. The neon-florescent tubes glowed, fully functional in the fixtures above. There wasn't even the faintest sign of a flicker. It was giving off a false sense of anti-climactic stillness. We reached the bottom step as the final floor spread out into a square beneath us. It was obvious that the hall through the door was just as well-lit as the stairwell; completely destroying the possibility of a monster boss level in the dark dungeon trope that I was expecting.

I couldn't really see any threats through the small window set into the door, but there was a whole lot more basement left for the wendigo to be lurking in. It was at that thought that I pulled out two of my "Everything" shotgun shells and swapped them with the rock-salt shells that I had loaded into my sawed-off earlier. I wasn't sure if any of the components that they were made with would do any damage to a wendigo, but I was going to find out. The last wendigo that I had fought, I had prepared for ahead of time. I went into that conflict knowing what I was up against. This time around, I had a variety of ammo for a spread of enemies. And even though I hadn't expected some grouch spirits stuck in limbo, I had the ammo for them. Yet, I had left anything that had to do with incendiary ammunition back at our new base of operations.

"I suppose one of us should open the door and go through it already." I suggested passively, silently hoping the Rook or Vergil would step up and take the initiative before me.

"Indeed, one of us should." Vergil agreed. "I guess that I will do it."

"Move." Rook grunted as he shoved past me to push the door open with his shoulder.

He immediately took a defensive stance as he readied his own revolver for trouble. I noted that he was loading the silver bullets that I had made for him with a speed loader. I knew he was just as worried as I was, because Rook had always been skeptical of the idea of a silver bullet. He knew full well that ballistic science had actually proven that the common concept that everyone pictured when they thought of a silver bullet was complete bullshit. However, there was a simple way to achieve a silver bullet without destroying the rifling of the gun that you fired the round from. It was a simple matter of setting a tip of silver within the point of the lead core of the bullet. When fired, the silver would still heat up to the point of near molten form, but now it was encased in a wonderful lead wrapper ready to deliver the viscous metal into the vulnerable bits of the monster beneath the skin.

Rook's larger frame obscured my ability to see through the doorway, so when he gestured for the two of us to follow him through, we were taking a risk. Even with all of the various magical and supernatural glamours, disguises, and whatnot that Rook had been exposed to; illusions were still difficult for him to deal with. He had definitely grown in other areas with his capabilities, especially his instincts.

The man had an uncanny, almost sixth sense about when an enemy was within about ten feet of him. But anything that lay in wait any further than that, Rook was blind to. And a wendigo could very easily traverse the length of this hallway in a matter of breaths. Rook would maybe be able to fire off one round before the beast would be on us. Thankfully, there was nothing that was lying in wait as we all passed through the last walls between the three of us and the lair of the fiendish abomination that we planned to end this night.

Vergil stepped in front of me, standing shoulder to shoulder with Rook as we carefully began moving down the corridor. Much like the stairwell, everything seemed quiet and eerily empty. The few rooms that we passed were locked and we dared not attempt to break into. If you needed a pocket picked, I was your man. But if you needed a lock picked you had best check the Yellow Pages. The walls and floors were that off-color of white that hospitals seem to frequently use, causing the whole passage to practically glow in the florescent lighting.

That was until everything turned very wrong. As we reached the end of the first hallway, the white floors abruptly shifted to an off-shade of reddish-brown as the walkway forked in two opposite directions.

I took a quick glance down either direction, not knowing what to expect. Oddly, both ways were clearly illuminated, as the tube bulbs shined light from above on every detail animating the walkways into scenes from a terror-filled past. Four sweeping gouges were ripped out of the perfectly tiled floors. The coppery stain of dried blood painted the walls and ceiling in smears. Tattered patches of cloth littered the ground here and there, the color unidentifiable beneath the grime of dried carnage. A smell that was fouler than any of the other dens of wendigos that I had dealt with in the past wafted in the air. It was hard not to wretch as you could practically taste the stench permeating the air.

Not knowing which way was the better option; we decided to take the right fork and hoped for the best. It didn't take us long before we found another turn and another hallway full of rot and blood stained damage.

"So tell me more about wendigos." Rook requested, breaking the silence. "Knowledge is power, as you've proven, MacClaude."

"Well, they are more prominent in Native-American and indigenous North-American legends." I answered. I could tell that Rook was attempting to distract himself. "They actually pop up in other cultures and countries with different names all over the world. In Japan, they are called Jikininki. In places like India, China, and Vietnam they are called Preta. No matter what part of the world that they hale from, all of them started out as a human. All of the versions devour human flesh, and they are always vicious, monstrous killers."

"Ok…" Rook hummed. "That's enough history I think. What do they look like?"

"They are huge!" I replied. "Like I said earlier, they are a minimum of seven feet tall. Wendigos are gauntly pale, practically snow white. Their bones press into their skin, stretching it taunt over their devilish frames. Their limbs are unnaturally long and they grow claw-like digits that replace the tips of their fingers. Each one becomes the equivalent of a long, laser-sharp dagger. And then there are their eyes. They are sunk into their eye-sockets so deep that they are almost invisible. It gives them a damn right sinister look, which gets worse if their eyes catch any light source. When that happens, you can see two pale glowing orbs shining out from the black sockets."

"Oh goody! They sound like loads of fun!" Rook bemoaned. "Is there anything else that I should know about them that will help keep me alive?"

The sound of bare feet slapping on tile silenced the conversation immediately. The three of us immediately put our backs to one another's, facing out against the three open passageways in front of our individual lines of sight. The distant echoes of adolescent laughter danced in the air and reverberated all around us. It was soon accompanied by the noise of running feet again, but this time, it seemed like the footfalls came from a different direction.

"Yeah…" I answered through gritted teeth. "They are known to make sounds like screaming or laughing children and women while they're stalking they're prey."

"Great, what does that make us?" Rook growled raising his revolver to eye level.

"Big worms on a small ass hook!" I answered as I attempted to lift my own gun.

"That may be true, but let us not die here today." Vergil added. "Be at the ready gentlemen, it won't be long now."

"Hey Vergil," Rook commented, "do us all a favor and leave the pep talks to someone else."

I managed to let a laugh escape me as a look of confusion and then insult swept over Vergil's brow. I barely blinked my eyes to fight back any more laughter. It was a bad idea. The moment I opened them, I could see the outline of the wendigo at the end of the hall in front of me. It was standing at full height and deathly still. Its pale color was almost glowing against the dark shades of dried blood that stained the surfaces around it. The laughter immediately curdled into a lump of air in my throat, and I was only able to smack Rook and Vergil's arms lightly to get their attention.

"What is it MacClaude?!" Rook snapped swiveling his head to look at me. Apparently he saw the wendigo as well because he could barely respond. "Oh… that…"

"Am I to guess that it is in the hall in front of Danyael?" Vergil inquired, slowly turning around.

"Yeah," I stammered. "On the count of three, we book it down the hall in front of Rook. One… two…"

I didn't make it to three. Both Rook and Vergil were running, dragging me by my injured arm behind them. The sound of a child cackling in glee bounced in the air accompanied shortly by a bellow that sounded as if Hell itself was belching. As we reached the next turn in the hallway, the wendigo was gripping the corners on the wall, pulling itself with its sinewy muscles around the corner with little difficulty. The florescent illumination caught its eyes, giving it the illusion that its eyes were burning orbs of white fire. I lifted my gun again, trying to steady myself as my comrades yanked me around the next corner. It was a good thing that they had, because the wendigo then launched itself ferociously down the hall with the speed rivaled by few supernatural creatures. Its claws raked the wall wear my head had been just seconds before. A cloud of plaster and drywall exploded into the air behind us as that part of the wall disintegrated into nothingness beneath the wendigos attack. I kept my gun up as it came around the corner and let loose one round at it. The shot was good.

I could hear the creature hiss in irritation as its body jerked slightly where the blast struck it. Most creatures wouldn't have been able to survive a shot to the chest like that. Sadly, wendigos weren't most creatures. My attack was a minor annoyance equivalent to a bee sting at best. Sure, the blast hurt it; but not enough to stop it.

"Oh balls!" I shouted as I turned around, never stopping the forward movement of my feet. "You guys are up, you benched me, remember!?"

True to their word, they both shifted gears and went on the offensive. Rook took my place and began unloading his revolver into the wendigo at a rapid pace. For whatever reason, the silver seemed to hurt it a lot more than my "Everything" round. I watched as the silver-tipped bullets pierced the wendigos chest, causing it to scream. An awful wail of horrific noise sang out from its mouth. The wendigo threw its arms open, spreading the spears of its hands wide and threatening with their very existence. And while Rook was shooting it, Vergil was not idle. He had taken the bottle of alcohol and squirted a line from our position to the wendigo in a hurried fashion. Thankfully, we didn't need perfect, we needed functional.

Vergil then pulled a knife from his belt and stabbed a few holes into the bottle and then threw it at the wendigo. It was only by sheer chance that it had taken that particular moment to bare its chest in anger after Rook had emptied his revolver. The bottle struck the wendigo's sternum and splashed out in a glorious explosion of flammable fluid. Rook pulled out his lighter and flicked the lid open. He struck the wheel several times, desperately trying to get the wick to ignite.

"Shit, shit, shit!" Rook shouted in total terror and raw anger. "Just light damnit!"

That final demand was apparently the correct thing to say, because the flint finally struck a spark large enough to catch the wick on the lighter. A small plume of orange and blue trickled to life over the small metal lighter right before Rook tossed it at the line of alcohol on the floor. But as the lighter hit the fluid, the wendigo jumped towards us with blinding speed. Its body twisted in an inhuman motion as it slid over the flames that ignited on the ground. The beast cleared my head and barreled into Rook. The older man was sent tumbling down the hall. I flinched internally as I knew that he was probably unconscious after a blow like that. The creature turned to Vergil as a wicked grin spread from its thin lips.

To his credit, Vergil did not falter or faint. He lashed out with his knife, striking with quick decisive stabs. The wendigo, clearly not prepared for this, did not move as the blade peeled back its flesh where the blade sliced. I suspected that the blade was blessed or had some sort of holy enchantment on it to do that type of damage, because I distinctly remember my knives not doing shit to the wendigos that I had fought in the past.

Sadly, Vergil's fury of knife strikes was cut short. The wendigo managed to smack the knife out of Vergil's hand as he made a final sweep with the blade. It hit the floor and slid near my feet. I watched as Vergil attempted to dodge the wendigo as the beast swung its monstrous arms in a killing arc. Thankfully, the close quarters of the hallway were in our favor as its claws raked the ceiling, slowing its strike enough for Vergil to dodge it. I took this moment to drop and make a go for the blade. It was the only weapon that we had that seemed to do any damage to the wendigo, and I wasn't going to go down without a fight.

As I grasped for the knife I wound up shoving it closer to the fading flames on the floor. In my panicked attempt to pick the knife up, the blade moved directly into the line of flames and ignited itself. Realizing I had mere moments, I seized the handle and flung myself at the wendigo. I swung wildly with the blade, missing a killing blow entirely. But much like before, I didn't need a perfect blow, I just need close enough.

The flame on the blade jumped to the wendigos, decaying, alcohol drenched flesh with ease. Its white skin burst into flames in a matter of seconds. Another putrid wail escaped its maw as it began flailing. Vergil wasted no time and drop-kicked its chest towards the way it had come from. The smoldering alcohol on the floor had almost extinguished, but the moment the wendigos foot touched the flickering remains of our first attack, an eruption of inferno engulfed the creature from the floor.

I ran to Rook to make sure that he was ok. I could feel a pulse and see his chest rise and fall gently with breaths. I looked to his eyes and noted that they were open, but clearly unfocused and dazed. I gently slapped his cheek twice with a grim smile.

"Nap time is over old man." I jested weakly. "Get your lazy ass up."

"Oh crap, you're still alive." Rook groaned as he sat up slowly. "I was hoping the wendigo would eat you and rid me of your wise ass."

"Well the jokes on you." I laughed. "I can't die until my magical debt is fulfilled. And even then, I don't plan on dying until I get to put you in a nursing home."

"Hardy har har." Rook chortled. "So, we won?"

"Yes, Agent Hightower, we won." Vergil sighed as he backed toward us, never taking his eyes off the burning form of the wendigo. "I am glad that you are alive. Most men would not have survived such an attack."

"Yeah, well I spent my youth being knocked around on a football field for fun." Rook laughed. "I guess it gave me an edge here. And I thought that it would have no real world applications outside of the NFL."

I heard a loud pop within the smoldering remains of the wendigo, snapping my attention to its body collapsing in on itself. My stomach released as I realized I had been clenching it for an unknown amount of time. I offered Vergil his knife back, which he took gingerly. It disappeared within its sheath as he turned away from the wendigo for the first time.

"I believe we were down here for some thrilling heroics!?" Vergil spoke up.

"Vergil! Did you just try to quote Firefly?!" I asked whimsically. "I am so proud of you!"

"I figure this was a good win and you earned it." Vergil laughed. "But don't get used to it."

"You know MacClaude," Rook said as he stood up, "I think that you're finally getting through to him."

"I regret this immediately." Vergil sighed.

"You know, I think you're right?" I added. "So, shiny! It's time for some more thrilling heroics!"

Vergil just walked past us and made his way down the blood stained hallway. Rook and I followed behind him, snickering the whole time. You had to learn to laugh after nearly dying; otherwise, you would go insane. Hopefully finding Dawn wouldn't take too much longer. Hopefully…

CHAPTER 4
FUNERAL PYRE

It quickly became apparent that the basement level of this building was a nightmarish labyrinth. This was in part due the wendigo essentially painting the walls with the blood of its victims. That aside, there were no signs or direction, just the putrid stench from the dried blood and gore that decorated the halls and the occasional debris from gouges in the walls.

I was beginning to suspect that the reason that the wendigo had remained down here for so long had less to do with the ghosts being ass holes and more to do with the fact that it was unable to navigate its way ant better than we were currently faring.

"Christ on a cracker!" I shouted in frustration. "How in the hell did the Order find anything down here?!"

"Would you please refrain from using my younger brother's name so profanely?" Azrael asked out of nowhere, causing the three of us to jump. We all turned around almost in the same movement with our weapons drawn.

"Damnit Azrael, put a fricken bell on or something!" I bellowed, placing my hand on my chest. "You scared the crap out of us!"

"I apologize." Azrael commented. "I will make an effort to make my presence known in a less startling manner if you can put the effort to not take my father or brother's name in vain in company."

"Yeah, yeah, sure." I replied. "I take it that you're all done upstairs?"

"You would be correct in your assumptions." Azrael answered.

"Are you incapable of answering with a yes or no?" I scoffed.

"When dealing with the supernatural, you should know that you will never get a straight answer." Vergil laughed. "Now, my lord Azrael, we could use your assistance."

"What difficulties trouble you and your companions Danyael?" Azrael inquired.

The angel wasn't being rude and ignoring Vergil, he was just unable to speak to any mortal directly. The only reason that he was able to speak to me was because of a literal, magical loop hole that he had managed to exploit. It was all a tad too confusing to get into the details.

"We need your help locating Dawn." I replied. "We are running around in circles down here."

"Verily, this whole level has a spiritual curse on it." Azrael commented. "I would have been surprised if you had managed to find the exit."

"How long have you have known this?!" I asked irritably.

"Since the three of you first exited the stairway." Azrael answered. "I was preoccupied with my task and I knew that you all were more than capable of dispatching the wendigo. I had every intention of coming to aid you all when both of our labors were accomplished. And thus, here I am."

"I'll give you a pass on this." I growled. "But it would be nice if you could have shared this information sooner."

"Should have, could have... let's just get on with this!" Rook barked.

"I agree with Stephen." Vergil added. "Your complaints are juvenile and a waste of all of our time."

There was a sensation of the air growing tight against my skin followed by a mass flickering of the florescent lights. Then there was a popping feeling, like a plastic seal releasing pressure. And then it was over. In the time that it had taken for me to inhale and exhale, Azrael had transported all of us to an unknown part of the basement. The lights hummed at a different frequency as their glow pattered on and off. It was as if they were dancing to the rhythm of the electricity coursing through them. The air was colder, almost to the point of feeling damp. There were four doors in this new hallway, two on either side of the corridor, offset in their placement. At the end of the hall sat a desk with a lock box hanging on the wall above it.

"I surmised that for the sake of expediency, it would be easier to just move all of us here rather than continuing to bicker." Azrael announced. He walked to the end of the hall and began rifling through the desk, leaving us at the doors.

Rook, Vergil, and I each took a door and attempted to open them, and each of us failing to do so in turn. We all met at the final door and found it to be as secure as the other three. I slammed my fist against the door in frustration.

I hated shooting locks. It never worked like it did in the movies. And it would be next to impossible to attempt to kick the door in. We seemed to have reached a temporary impasse.

"Hey Azrael," I called over my shoulder as I stared daggers through the door in my mind, "do you think that you can work some sort of angel, mojo miracle here and get these doors open?"

"I can most assuredly open the doors." Azrael answered as he approached from down the hall. "But I will certainly not be using angel mojo miracles. That is simply absurd!"

"Fine," I snapped, "call it whatever you want. Magic, miracles, the Force! Just ope…"

"How about the guard's keys?" Azrael asked, jingling the brass keys by my ears. I distinctly heard Vergil snicker under his breath and Rook snort to stifle laughter. "I thought that you knew that magic is rarely the correct answer.

"Out of all of the angels that could have possibly…" I grumbled. "Give me the damn keys.

Azrael obliged, dropping the keys into my hand. From there, I went about opening the doors. The first one revealed a barren room with padded walls and a single toilet built into the floor. The second door opened into much of the same. The third however had a decaying corpse bundled in the corner. Its gender was unidentifiable. Words of madness were scribbled on the walls in a coppery shade, offering any who dared to read a glimpse into this poor bastard's mind as they suffered until their death.

The final room was the most difficult to take in. The fact that there was an actual, live person imprisoned inside made it so much more deplorable. The floors and walls were padded much the same as the previous rooms had been, however that is where the similarities ended. Where the other rooms had white walls and floors, this room's color was obscured with filth. There was a toilet like the others, but it was bent up and covered in the same film of grime that coated the floor and walls. The lights fixtures above were barely lit; at least the few of them that hadn't burned out. Their pale glow gave the room and eerie and depressing ambiance.

And sitting huddled against the far wall opposite of the door was a malnourished female; almost as androgynous as the corpse from the neighboring room. Her hair was draped over her entire body, covering her exposed flesh, but just barely. I could not tell you what color that it was, only that it was matted with filth and that it was easily long enough to reach her waist in its current state. The woman's skin was so pale that it seemed whiter than the cell's normal palette. Her flesh clung to her features so much that she could have been mistaken for a very small wendigo. At least that was until you met her eyes.

It wasn't just their abnormally colored irises, or the fact that they seemed to almost glow like the eyes of a cat. No, a fire that I can only have described as akin to a blazing vortex of destruction burned into everything that her gaze fell upon. Even in her clearly weakened state, an air of pride and power emanated from the very air around her. Through the refuse, various odors, and obvious signs of torture that this woman had endured, she had never allowed herself to break.

I approached her very slowly, allowing her head to lift feebly and take in my presence. I carefully avoided eye contact with her as I took a knee next to her hobbled form. I noticed her eyes closed as a single tear managed to escape her strength and free itself.

"Dawn?" I asked. She nodded her head slowly. "I'm Danny, I am the guy that spoke to you before. We are going to get you out of here."

I shifted my body and began to take my coat off so that she could have something more than her own hair to cover herself with. I realized that she was attempting to speak to me, as her mouth began trembling and trying to open very slowly. Her lips quivered with effort, as a low, rasping croak escaped from her mouth that I didn't understand.

"Try that again, I didn't catch what you said." I instructed softly. "Take it slow."

"I… said…" Dawn gasped hoarsely as she inhaled, "it's… about… damn… time."

I froze not knowing how to react to this or what to say. This was odd, because I always had sass to spare. But then again, I had never been great with speaking to women, let alone fae women. Hell, most of my conversations with Nisa had been complete fiascos, and she was half human. I won't even waste your time telling you about the bitch that was the Queen of the Seelie Court. An elf was entirely new territory for me.

"Stop staring like an idiot." Dawn croaked, clearly a bit more collected than before, "Now pick me up, I cannot walk in my current state."

"Oh, right." I snapped out of my mind and draped my coat over her lithe body before coiling my arms under her frame. I lifted her as carefully as I could. Despite how frail and light her body was, it was an awkward undertaking.

"You kind of suck at this hero thing." Dawn rasped in a chuckle.

"I'm not a hero. At least not usually." I added. "I'm usually the ass hole who does the crap that no one likes to mention, or I just rip off rich idiots."

"That explains so much." Dawn laughed in a whisper as she nodded into unconsciousness.

I lifted my head and looked towards my friends for the first time since I had entered the cell. All of them were staring intently, each with a different expression on their face. Vergil wore his over-serious, judgmental facial tick. Azrael looked concerned yet distant, as if his mind were elsewhere. Which it probably was. And then there was Rook. FBI Special Agent Stephen-fucking Hightower had the biggest, shit-eating grin spread ear to ear, painted on his grizzled mug.

"What?!" I asked as I cautiously made my way to the door. "What are you all staring at?"

"Oh, nothing." Rook replied.

"Shut up!" I warned.

"I didn't say anything." Rook exclaimed.

"You were thinking it." I declared as I attempted to ignore Rook's obvious amusement.

"Does anyone else notice that Danyael's injuries seem to have stopped bothering him?" Vergil observed as he stepped aside to allow me to exit.

"Let's just get out of here." I groaned. "Azrael, can you be a pal?"

"Are you requesting that I transport all of you out of the building?" the arch angel asked. "If so, please be specific in your future requests."

"Ok, sure." I growled. "Just do the thing and get us out of here."

Azrael made a noise that sounded almost like a grunt of disapproval. I ignored him and turned my attention to Dawn, preparing myself for the sensation that accompanied Azrael's power. I had learned that the further the distance of travel, the more intense the sensory overload that was caused by his feat. I almost held my breath waiting for it to begin, worry and anticipation were the only things that kept my focus. I closed my eyes and exhaled, wondering why Azrael was taking so long.

The sounds of the night practically exploded in greeting. I opened my eyes to discover that all of us were standing in the front drive of the building.

The noise of passing vehicles on the road in the distance bleated into the emptiness of the night. I was stunned to see how much time had passed since entering the building. We had begun mid-morning. It was now night. I felt Dawn stir in my arms, so I looked down to see if she was alright. I found her staring darkly at the structure in front of us. Vergil and Rook had begun discussing something about assisting someone else, but I didn't catch the details. My attention was fixated on the raw hatred spilling out from Dawn towards her former prison.

No… not the prison. Dawn's rage was for the Order of Saint Patrick. Her growing wrath washed over me, mirroring my own that I had harbored for so long. Dawn's hatred awoke my deep seated fury and I felt power surge throughout every fiber of my being. Azrael's words from earlier whispered in the dark of my mind. Only fire can undo the stain. My heart began to race as I repeated the words to myself. I wanted to burn the Order to the ground and this was a great start. The irony of using fire to destroy them did not escape me. They had made an enemy of me by burning my mother alive. Now they would come to regret that decision. My father would regret his decision.

Dawn looked up at me, intensifying the entanglement of our emotions. I became aware that she knew that I was getting ready to do something destructive, because a look of approval and glee played across her face and blended in with our mutual hatred. I nodded to her and we both returned our attention to the doomed building. I raised my hand and let Dawn's malice mix with the energy coursing through me. I let it guide the magic within me, the spoils of my encounter with the dark wizard Aleister Crowley. I had never attempted to use this power intentionally. When I had used it in the past, it had always been purely instinctual or in moments of pure emotion. Now I wanted it. I demanded that the magic answer my call. And so it did.

I willed the power reach out and grab the structure. It did as instructed. My mind commanded that the building burn. It screamed for it. And my magic made it so. I felt æther pull through the Veil, igniting the cement foundation of the structure. My rage entwined with Dawn's flooded into the æther-fueled flames, igniting them into a blend of white and blue that seeped into every nook and cranny of the effigy of our hate. In seconds, a roaring inferno was dancing skyward, feeding on the would-be stronghold.

"Danyael, what are you doing?!" I heard Vergil shout from behind me. "There were still people in the building."

"No, there were no people in that building." I answered coolly. "There were murderers and monsters, but there were no people."

"That's not your call to make, MacClaude!" Rooked shouted. But instead of anger, his voice rang with sorrow.

"Then whose is it?!" I snapped back. "Who holds them accountable when the rest of the world doesn't know a damn thing about what they do? Or they don't want to know and conveniently turn a blind eye."

"You have sinned in your life too, Danyael." Vergil accused. "What makes you any better than them?! What gives you the right?!"

"She does!" I shouted as I lifted Dawn up higher. "My mother does. Every innocent fae and human who the Order has harmed… You are still lucky that I haven't riddled you with buckshot. The Order kills without remorse; I am just leveling the playing field."

I turned to see Azrael staring at me blankly. His stoic expression made it impossible to tell if he was judging me or not. I wanted to scream at him. To tell him to show some sign of emotion. I couldn't stand his indifference.

"Do you have something that you'd like to contribute?!" I spat.

"Danyael, calm yourself." Azrael encouraged. "I do not agree nor disagree with your actions or your statement. Those men inside were due to die this night. If you were not destined to be the one to end them, I know not who would have. Nonetheless, they perished. And they did so with sin staining their souls. Now I have a job to do, excuse me."

"Let's get out of here." I ordered. I did not wait for Vergil or Rook to argue with me.

CHAPTER 5
READING BETWEEN THE LINES

Azrael completed whatever it was that he did when he performed his duties as the Angel of Death. After that, he had taken all of us back to our base of operations where he began the task of healing Dawn in what limited ways that he was capable of. Biblical figures and the fae typically didn't agree with one another.

Our base was an out of place castle in the Northern California countryside that we had borrowed after its previous occupant had been taken by the Order of Saint Patrick. It had all of the modern amenities and perks, plus it was isolated and way out of the way. The closest city was nearly an hour away. It was the perfect place for us to transport in and out of without risking the chance that someone would see us vanishing into thin air. Vergil and Rook had remained uncharacteristically silent since we had returned. Rook was sitting at his laptop, clicking his mouse on occasion as he absently went about distracting himself. His reality-hardened face was lined with frustration and worry. Vergil, sat in one of the high-backed armchairs left by the previous owner, staring into space. His face was intense yet blank.

It was safe to say that there was clear tension in the air radiating from the two of them. And it was beginning to grate on my nerves. I cleared my throat to try and initiate some sort of response from either of them. Of course, both remained fixated on what they were doing and ignored me completely. This in turn, only made me angrier.

"Do either of you want to get something off of your chests?" I asked loudly, shattering the silence.

"I do, but I won't right now." Rook answered with a deep huff. "I am having trouble processing my thoughts as it stands. The cop in me wants to arrest you here and now for that stunt. But knowing everything that I do… I just need time to think. When Azrael is done, I'm going to have him take me home."

"I will be requesting my temporary leave with Lord Azrael as well." Vergil added. "I have much to contemplate. Where was the line between justice and murder tonight? Where do we draw the line in the future?"

"Whatever." I chided. "I wasn't wrong, nor will I apologize for what I did."

"Danny, I'm not disagreeing with your stance, per say," Rook said as he stood up, "but we need to do things differently than our enemies, otherwise we are no better than they are."

A muted hush fell on the room as the three of us simply stared at each other. I knew that Rook wasn't attacking me, and a part of me agreed that we should be doing things differently than our enemies. Especially in regards to the Order of Saint Patrick. Yet, I also felt that what I had done was justified. There likely would not have been any chance to save the Brethren of the Order that had been left in the building when it went up in flames. Their minds had been broken beyond recovery long before we had arrived there looking for Eve. Not to mention the many atrocities that they had knowingly committed in the name of their faith.

No, they had earned their fate. However, I would definitely try to heed Rook's words from here on out. He was the only friend that I had left and I didn't want to lose him. Vergil was an ally, sure, but he and I would never be friends of any sort. And then there was Azrael… Whatever thought that I had been forming, vanished as the angel entered the room as if on cue. His expression and demeanor was neutral and exhausted.

"I have done what I can for her." Azrael announced. "She will need to eat to maintain her health. I was able to heal the malnutrition, but without sustenance, her body will still fail."

"What do you mean by that?" I asked.

"Think of it like rewinding a video tape." Azrael explained. "If you do so too many times, eventually the tape wears out and snaps. Due to the extent of the damage that she has suffered, this was the final rewind. I expect that she used her own magic and natural abilities to heal herself during her captivity. Otherwise, she would have perished long ago."

"Any recommendations of what she needs immediately?" I asked.

"A shower and rest. I have already taken the liberty of bringing her the immediate nutrition that her body needs. "Azrael answered. "She was eating and preparing for a shower when I left her. Now, I believe that I am needed to take your associates home."

"Yeah, if you don't mind?" Rook added.

"Danyael, please take caution in my absence." Azrael warned. "Dawn is a creature of magic. You are well aware of the ways of the fae. Be vigilant."

"Yeah, I know." I replied. "But I don't think that she's going to be a threat."

"Not in the ways that you would expect." Azrael commented. "Your's and the elf's fates are now entangled, yet all I am able to foresee in any future is pain."

"Life is pain." I quoted. "Anyone who says otherwise is trying to sell something."

Azrael held up his hands in surrender as he approached Vergil. His eyes never left me as he motioned for Rook to join him. Rook made his way past me, stopping briefly to pat my shoulder and back reassuringly. I gave Rook a grin and hit his stomach with the back of my hand. He returned a feeble smile as he stepped in front of Azrael.

"See you in a few… take care, MacClaude." Rook said.

"You better not smoke more than one pack of cigarettes while you're gone." I told my older friend.

"Screw you." Rook laughed. "I am a grown-ass man. I will smoke however many that I want."

Rook gave me a final wave, and then there was a flicker in the lighting, followed by what I could only describe as the sounds of wings flapping. It seemed so cliché given that Azrael was an angel, but I call things as they are. This had been the first time that I had been this close to Azrael as he used his abilities without having him use them on me as well. By the time that I had made the connection, the three of them had vanished. In the absence of their company, the deafening silence was unsettling, so I resolved myself to check on Dawn. We had decided to put her up in the master bedroom because it had its own bathroom.

I made my way up the stairs, rolling Azrael's warning over and over in my mind. I knew little to nothing about elves, other than they were near extinct and that they could touch iron, unlike the majority of the fae races. I wanted to remedy my ignorance, causing many questions to fester in my mind. Each one growing in demand as I neared the entrance to the bedroom.

I came upon the open door, causing my mind to evacuate all thoughts and enter into panic mode. I pulled my gun, steadying it in front of me and entered the room cautiously. My eyes began scanning the chamber as my stomach clenched in anticipation. I heard the patter of muffled footsteps and I turned to face it with my weapon raised.

"Is that a gun, or are you just happy to see me." Dawn asked as she walked past me casually. She held a pair of scissors in her hand, causing a phantom pain to assault my shoulders. She was wearing one of Eve's black, silk robes, but more out of practicality and less for the aesthetics. But it was still difficult for me to tell that difference. "Put the gun down, Tex. Everything is fine. I just went to find some scissors to cut the matted locks out of my hair."

"Oh, I'm sorry." I said, letting my gun drop into its holster. "I've been through a lot of weird crap, so I'm a bit paranoid."

"You're ok." Dawn laughed as she made her way to the bathroom. "If you hadn't figured it out, I'm an elf, I am used to weird."

"Yeah, about that," I questioned as my curiosity piqued again, "you're not what I was expecting. Would you mind telling me more about your people?"

"My people?" Dawn mused, stepping into the bathroom and leaving the door slightly ajar. I walked over and leaned against the adjacent wall. "If you are asking me about elves, I only know what my mother and father told me as a child before they left me with my rez-mom."

"Rez-mom?" I inquired.

"Reservation mom." Dawn answered. "The woman that my biological parents left me with. Her and her husband took me in and raised me after my parents left. They were good people and deserved better than what happened to them."

"I'm sorry." I replied solemnly. "I empathize with you. The Order has taken a lot from me as well."

"Well, I don't want to hear your tragic back-story that turned you into the gun-slinging, craptacular excuse for a hero that you are today." Dawn sighed as the sound of shears snipped off and on. "As far as elves go, they are nothing like what most people think of them. Much like dwarves, we are able to handle iron and steel. Unlike dwarves, we resemble the high fae in more ways than just aesthetics. The magic that elves wield is nearly equal to that of the high fae. That is one of the many reasons that they despise us so much."

"Oh, I know their prejudice well." I inserted. "I was indebted to the Queen of the Seelie Court for a while."

"Damn, that sucks to be you." Dawn scoffed. The buzz of an electric shaver turned on, making me puzzle how much of the castle had she managed to go through. "Anyways, like I was saying… elves are not as long lived as the high fae. We age similar to human until our twenties give or take. Then, sometime between our twentieth and thirtieth year, our aging slows down drastically. It takes about fifty human years for us to age one. It is true that elves love nature, but we also love convenience, invention, and ingenuity. This was why we were able to co-exist with humans so amiably. And another reason the high fae of the Courts hated us."

"So, Tolkien got it wrong?" I replied almost dejectedly. "Dang…"

"Great, you're a nerd." Dawn chuckled. "He didn't get it right, that's for sure. From what I have been told, elves never looked down on humans or hated dwarves. At least not in any way different than humans do each other. If people behaved ignorantly, we treated them as such."

"That's probably what caused the skewed ideas about elves." I observed. "Humans hate when anyone points out their faults. Especially when they are wrong."

"Well whatever the reason, it doesn't matter now." Dawn sighed. The buzzing noise clicked off. "What's done is done. I wasn't around for that."

"Well what are you going to do now?" I asked. "Where do you plan on going from here?"

"I don't know yet." Dawn answered, opening the bathroom door.

Dawn's hair was now cut in a short, punk-pixie style. It suited her angular face, which was fuller than it had been when I removed her from her prison. Sadly it still showed signs of her incarceration. Her hair color was an almost translucent, silvery-blonde that faded behind her tapered ears. Her eyes were an odd and eerie shade of lavender ice with dark shadowed crescents hanging beneath. Her lips were full but chapped. She seemingly paid me no mind as she made her way over to the closet. I studied her features closely as she opened the door and looked inside.

"So, what's a girl to wear?" Dawn asked as she stepped inside. "You are aware of how weird it is that there are so many women's clothes in here, yet the only other people that I have seen here have been the three men and the angel. Does one of you have a secret life? Is it you?"

"No," I blurted as I felt my face heat up. "Those belonged to the last owner of the castle. I just haven't found the time to go about getting rid of them."

"Yeah, uh-huh, I believe that." Dawn teased as she turned around to face me with a coy smile. "If that's true, why haven't you had one of the other guys to get rid of them?"

"The other two don't stay here with me." I answered. "Rook has a place of his own and I don't know or care where Vergil stays. On that note, neither of them is here. They left a few minutes ago."

"Really now?" Dawn asked, cocking an eyebrow inquisitively. "So you're telling me that we are the only ones here right now?"

"Well... yeah." I answered slowly. "Why?"

"Well you see, Mister Hero..." Dawn replied as she made her way to me. She grabbed my hand and yanked me off the wall. I staggered forward and wound up face to face with her. "I've been alone for a long time and I have and itch that absolutely needs to be scratched. Oh, and of course you need your reward for your heroic deeds."

"Oh... um..." I fumbled my words as I realized what her intentions were. "But I'm not a hero."

"Then don't question your good fortune." Dawn whispered with her face so close to mine that I could feel the humidity of her breath. "Just don't read too much into this."

I felt the silk from the robe brush against my hand as it fell to the floor. I could feel my pulse race as Dawn placed her hand against my chest and guided me until I felt the edge of the bed touch the backs of my knees. Her coy smile transformed into a playfully wicked grin as I resigned to my fate.

CHAPTER 6
OUTSIDE INTERFERENCE

The last thing that Rook had expected to find when he checked in at the Roseville office of the FBI was a case waiting for him on his temporary desk. His prolonged presence in California was making things appear a bit too permanent to the office brass. Rook had known that it was only a matter of time before the higher-ups started taking advantage of having him localized. He had just picked up that case file when the sounds of footsteps approaching made him turn around reflexively.

"Hightower!" Division Head Ditco barked. "I'm glad that you're back."

"Sir," Rook nodded. "Is this about the case file on my desk?"

"Yes it is." Ditco affirmed, opening his own copy of the file. "This has been shared with us from our European liaison; I believe that you have met Agent Phineas MacClaude?"

"Yes, sir." Rook answered mechanically. "It was a brief encounter, but I remember it well. How can I be of service to our European allies?"

"Well, it seems that an organization that has roots in Europe has set up camp in Northern California. The Redding area specifically. While the group was based overseas, every metropolitan area that they had operated in eventually wound up with a mass of missing persons."

"Ok sir…" Rook reflected, "So why was this case given to me? I am happy to help, but this isn't the typical case that gets thrown my way."

"You have a solid reputation for cracking impossible cases and nailing down culprits." Ditco hummed as he flipped through the contents of the file. "Aside from the Danny Nimbus case that is. That being said, this case isn't quite so cut and dry. All of the missing persons tended to be loners and solitary people. By the time the first report was even filed, the suspect organization has packed up and moved on. They maintain plausible deniability and continue on with their operations."

"Isn't the fact that they are constantly moving their headquarters suspect enough to at least get something to bring them in?" Rook asked, his interest piqued.

"And that there is the snag." Ditco sighed, snapping the folder closed. "This organization, Bethlehem, is a homeless out-reach organization. They operate in cities and metropolitan areas with high transient populations, yet never in any high-profile areas or cities. They invest in local real estate, buying properties and buildings and developing some of them into low-income housing. Yet they never actually lease these apartments out, and they never quite finish the low-income buildings. Instead they tie up their supposed resources and end up selling the properties to bigger companies from larger cities. They always turn a profit, and between the money they use to buy off city councils as well as State and Government officials, and the public work that they actually perform, everyone seems to turn a blind eye to their comings and goings."

"What about the homeless population?" Rook inquired. "Are any of the missing persons from the homeless community?"

"Not as far as sources can confirm." Ditco answered. "In fact, the homeless situation usually improves after Bethlehem leaves an area. Their numbers drop and the cities look better for it."

"Why not assign the B. A. U. on this?" Rook asked. "This seems more of their type of case."

"They're currently preoccupied with another case." Ditco replied. "But rest assured, they will be joining you as soon as they are done. We're not going to have any issues with you taking this are we?"

"No sir." Rook affirmed. "I'm just gathering any and all details."

"Good, I want you on this immediately!" Rook's superior snapped. "Don't drop the ball on this. I don't want a screw up like your Danny Nimbus fiasco tied to this office. Prove to me that I am right about you and that your hype isn't just tall tales."

Ditco left before he was even able to open his mouth to respond. He left Rook in the Spartan office struggling to think up a plan of action. It wasn't that fact that he minded the work that was giving him pause, because he didn't. In fact, catching the mundane, human bad-guys might be a nice change from the monsters, angels, and fairy creatures. Rook just had to figure out how to keep the Behavioral Analysis Unit from finding out about Danny when they eventually joined up with him.

Eve's castle was about fourteen miles West of Redding, and his idiot friend didn't know the meaning of subtle or low-key. Hell, the moron was still holed up in a damn castle. One of his greatest enemies, the Order of Saint Patrick knew of the location of this same castle. And then, realization bitch-smacked Rook so hard his ears rang.

This case had been passed to the FBI by Phineas MacClaude, who was in fact a leading member of the Order of Saint Patrick. Danny, Vergil, and he had been putting in some painfully long nights searching for Eve, a sorceress that they had captured because she was pregnant with the nephilim offspring of Azrael, the Archangel of Death. If Rook was a betting man, he would put money on the fact that this was clearly an attempt to distract and tie Rook's hands and keep Danny dodging the FBI. If he was correct, it was an ingenious plan, which pissed Rook off to no end.

"I suppose that I should be grateful that the bastard hasn't sold me out to brass." Rook grumbled under his breath.

He sighed inwardly. Rook had recently discovered that the Redding area was notorious for being ludicrously hot in the summer. So this case was going to be the furthest from pleasant. He grabbed the case file from his desk to familiarize himself with the details as his free hand moved to his pocket for his cell phone. He tapped the screen and went through the process of unlocking it, and then absently tapped the screen until he was flicking through his contacts, searching for the one named, "Pain in my Ass." Almost as a reflex, he nearly tapped the call button. Thankfully he caught himself, and tapped the text message option instead.

This was definitely not the place to call a wanted fugitive. Instead, Rook furiously fumbled out a quick message that read, "We have a PROBLEM!" He quietly hit the send button as he pulled the case file to his chest. It looked like Rook would be driving back to Danny, and without Air-Angel to jump him there, it was going to be a long drive.

CHAPTER 7
A MOMENT'S PEACE

I had lost track of how long that Dawn and I had been laying in bed conversing. The world had seemed to fall away as we spoke to each other, and for the first time in a long while, I felt truly at ease. Dawn and I seemed to have connected over our mutual traumas, as we both took turns recanting the horrors of our pasts.

We had nary touched one another since we had been carnally entangled for what seemed like ages ago. It was the oddest thing, the two of us simply laid in bed, talking and reminiscing, with no pressure between either of us to do more and possibly make this moment awkward. After we had taken a few moments to regain our wits, Dawn had simply struck up a conversation that I felt comfortable enough to share with her. From that moment on, everything else seemed to be trivial, background noise.

"So, what's up with you and that Rook guy? You guys travel around killing ghosts and monsters?"Dawn inquired. "That sounds like a cliché comic book plot."

"More or less…" I answered. "Technically, I had been doing it on my own for two years before Rook took the case and tried to arrest me."

"Wait," Dawn interrupted, "What do you mean, 'arrest' you?!"

"Shit… let me back up." I answered. "When the Order of Saint Patrick killed my mom and burned our home to the ground, they made it appear to be an act of arson. Unbeknownst to me my mother had taken out a hefty, home owner's insurance policy as well as a sizeable life insurance policy, which was completely out of character for her. In everything that she had done since my dad left us, how could I have known that she would pre-pay for any type of insurance policy. I mean, she practically blew every spare cent that she had on booze and cigarettes. That being said, the police caught up with me and made it clear that I was their prime suspect and that they were going pin the whole thing on me. Thankfully a friend of mine broke me out of custody and after that I went on to sort of save the world from the escaped, disembodied soul of an extremely powerful dark wizard."

"Look at you doing Harry Potter's job for him!" Dawn mocked.

"Ha ha…" I smiled and threw a pillow at her. "Sadly, this story doesn't stop there. A war broke out amongst the Courts of the Fae, and since I had managed to put myself in debt to the Queen of the Seelie Court herself during the saving the world debacle, I was dragged into the middle of it. I helped the Queen dispatch her enemies who crossed my path and I got to stop a lot of the fae who prey on humans."

"I should really get some popcorn for this story." Dawn laughed.

"Do you want me to finish?" I growled playfully. She nodded with a smirk, so I continued. "Unfortunately, during my crusade against the fae and other creatures that go bump in the night, I racked up some property damage on an overwhelming scale for over two years. My guess is that the Order helped put that fact in the sights of the FBI, which eventually branded me as a mass-arsonist as well as a murder. "

I took a moment to recall everything that I had been through since then, and it was daunting to even attempt to think about. I almost asked myself how I had managed to drag my sorry ass through everything since then, but I noticed that Dawn was looking at me expectantly.

"I remained uncaught and off the radar, which the boys at the Bureau did not like at all." I continued as I put a pin in that thought for later. "Apparently it's bad PR for a wanted fugitive to elude the FBI for so long after walking out of police custody. It didn't help that I was a street magician before I got sucked into all of this. Eventually, my case got passed to Special Agent Stephen Hightower, or as you know him, Rook. Apparently he had built himself a reputation on solving the impossible cases. Oddly enough, many of his cases were tied to the very same crap that I had began to fight against, he just didn't know it."

"Is that how you convinced him to work with you?" Dawn questioned skeptically. "Because from where I am standing, that is a huge jump away from his job description. I mean, we're talking Grand Canyon sized leaps away."

"Would you believe me if I told you that it was divine intervention?" I asked. Dawn answered the question with an incredulous glare. "Yeah, I didn't think that you would. But, that's what happened… kind of. Both Rook and I wound up meeting Odin, the Allfather and ruler of the Aesir Gods."

You gotta be kidding me?!" Dawn laughed in disbelief. "Both of you met an Old God? But not just any god, but Odin. As in Wotan, or Ol' One-Eye? Tell me, did he look like Anthony Hopkins?"

"No, smart ass, he didn't." I retorted. "Actually, he looked more like the guy in the rain coat on that fish sticks box. Except, he wore a Vikings football hat. And if you want to get technical, I've not only met Odin, but I am friends with a pretty popular demi-god."

"Now you are just bragging." Dawn said snidely. "Go ahead and tell me who. Is it Heracles. Oh wait, he eventually became a god."

"Actually his name is Bromerys, son of the Celtic God, Cernunnos." I replied. I could almost feel the old Stag's energy as I spoke his name with such familiarity. Apparent;y, so did Dawn. Her mocking chuckles ceased as her eyes began searching around the room expectantly.

"Did you feel that?!" She asked carefully.

"Yeah, I did." I answered. "I haven't seen Bromerys in a while, but he has pulled me out of some dark places. But I digress. One of those fae who had rebelled against the Queen of the Seelie Court had somehow convinced the ice giants of Jotunheim to cooperate with him and he attempted to stage a coup. He offered them dominion here and had them attack Midgard, in exchange for their help overthrowing the Courts of Fae once they conquered Midgard. He swayed them by pointing out to the giants that the Old God's held now power in the realm of mortals any more. Somehow Rook and I met up in the chaos of all of this, and it's kind of difficult to arrest anybody when literal giants are wreaking havoc in New York City. To bring this long story to an abrupt end, I broke into the Order of Saint Patrick's Upstate New York Headquarters, stole Odin's Spear from their 'Blasphemous Artifact Vault,' and lost a close friend of mine in the process. In the end, we got the spear to Odin, fought the ice giants together, and bonded over him murdering the same fae who orchestrated the whole cake of bullshit."

"I'm having a little trouble taking all of this in." Dawn said quietly.

"Once Rook had been exposed to the world of magic, he caught on how things truly are real quick." I continued. "He realized the battles that we do with the things that go bump in the night and the various magical things that we combat typically has some collateral damage, usually in the form of burning or destroyed structures."

"Well, I can believe that part at least." Dawn stated after allowing a momentary, odd silence to settle. "So, now do you work with the FBI?"

"If only!" I sighed. "I am still a wanted criminal."

"Wait," Dawn interrupted again, "I thought that you said that you fought the ice giants with Rook in New York. Shouldn't the FBI be lining up to kiss your ass right about now? There has to be a record of that somewhere."

"Here's the part where I decided to do the noble hero thing for the first time in my life." I answered bitterly. "I knew that the world wasn't… isn't ready to know the truth about what lies beyond the Veil. They can't even get over something as stupid as race. Hell, there's a whole cult of Bible-black zealots who do know and they try to kill everything about it."

I took a deep breath and released it in a huff. I didn't want to cloud this happy moment with such negative concepts, but it seemed unavoidable.

"Like I said," I said sourly, "the world is still hung up on skin color and gender identity. Imagine what would happen if the whole lot of them learned that there are whole realms of people that are the furthest thing from their small-minded, misconceived concept of normal. No, I had Odin erase the knowledge and memory of pretty much everyone on Earth who had discovered the world that we live in through those events. Sure, I'm still a wanted criminal, but I know that I am capable of living that way. Having connections of any kind and doing what I do can get me and them killed. And even though I am on a first name basis with the Angel of Death, I still don't like to tempt fate."

"Your life is way more messed up than it seems." Dawn said as she stretched across the bed like a cat.

"You're not wrong." I laughed nervously.

I looked over at Dawn's now prone form at the foot of the bed. She returned the glance with an accusatory grin that caused me to erupt into laughter. Nothing that I had disclosed or that we had discussed prior had been humorous. Yet Dawn shared in my laughter as we filled the room with a chorus of our macabre amusement. After a few minutes, we allowed a hush to gently settle before either of us made a peep. Finally Dawn rolled out of bed and made her way back to the bathroom.

"You know, you seem like a lot of fun despite the tragic back story." Dawn said as she turned to face me. "I think that I will stick around for time being. Now get up, we need to shower. You need to take me to get some actual clothes. I will be damned if I'm going to be caught in one of those ridiculous dresses in that wardrobe. It's one thing to be an elf, but I refuse to wear an outfit that looks like it was borrowed from a Tim Burton movie villain."

I started laughing again as I stood up and followed her path to the bathroom. I had no idea what was in store for me if Dawn hung around, but for the first time in the last couple of years, I really didn't give a damn. And that felt peaceful.

CHAPTER 8
UNWANTED PRAYERS

Dawn had managed to convince me to hit up every thrift store we could find. Apparently she had a thing for clothes that had memories, or so she said. Currently, we were at the Salvation Army in Redding, with me being a pack mule for her intended purchases and her perusing the many racks of women's apparel. At one point, Dawn literally vanished inside the center of an over filled circular rack. This whole experience was very new to me. I had never really gone shopping like this, let alone with someone else. My mom had always bought her own garments when I wasn't around, and up until recently, the Queen of the Seelie Court had been having my clothing cleaned, altered, and repaired as needed so I hadn't thought about it in a while. My motto was, have coat and hat, will travel.

"Have you ever thought about branching out of the whole creepy magician look?" Dawn asked, poking her head out from the depths of the miniature jungle of clothing. "I mean, I understand that those clothes were part of your act when you were a street magician, but I thought you are trying to stay unnoticed. Aren't you supposed to not draw attention to yourself?"

"Oh, I forgot to let you in on a secret about this coat and hat." I said almost gleefully. "They are enchanted. They screw with technology and make normal humans not notice me. It is how I've managed to go undetected for as long as I have. Truth be told, I'm not that great with being stealthy and low-key."

"I couldn't guess." Dawn gasped sarcastically. "I mean you fricken live in a castle. And drive a Gremlin. How has that thing not broken down yet?"

"Magic." I laughed. "Apparently gremlins can build and repair things just as well as they can destroy and sabotage them."

"Your mechanic is a gremlin?" Dawn asked worriedly.

"Not one, several." I answered. "They work for the Queen and because I was in service to her, they have sworn to maintain my vehicle for as long as I am alive."

"I guess they figured that wasn't too long of a time to worry, seeing as you're mortal." Dawn mused.

I chuckled in response as she emerged from within the fabric foliage of her confinement. She was wearing a black denim vest that had once been a long coat over a white tank top, black and white leopard print, cut-off jean shorts, and black biker boots. The whole look seemed very rock-star and not very elf-like.

"What do you think?" Dawn asked as she struck a pose to model her newfound outfit.

"What eighties rock star did you kill and skin to find those shorts?" I joked loudly.

Dawn made a face of mock-offence and smacked me in the stomach with the back of her hand. She crossed her arms and gave me a stern scowl.

"What's with the cynicism?!" Dawn asked with a playful hiss. "Not Rivendell enough for you? I'm going to break it to you now, I'm not that type of elf. Think of me as if the movie version of Arwen was a biker."

"There's an image for the fan boys." I laughed.

"Pot and kettle, Danny, pot and kettle." Dawn teased. "Now let's get out of here and get something to eat. I haven't had real food in so long."

I nodded in agreement and we took her purchases up to the cash register. The young, male cashier stood in awe of Dawn as she counted out money that I had given her. The boy took no notice of me, but I wasn't sure if it was because of the effects of my hat and coat or Dawn herself. The poor idiot took a slow and careful pace bagging up the clothing, staring at her the entire time his hand worked. Eventually Dawn took notice of the cashier noticing her and she cocked her eyebrow in disapproval.

"Advert your eyes, Sport, it will never happen." Dawn said, crushing the poor sod's soul, heart, and confidence with a single sentence.

"Owe!" I flinched for the poor guy, as we both turned and left him slumped at his register. "Man, you whammied him hardcore! Do elves have an attraction glamour?"

"Not exactly." Dawn answered quietly. "All elves, even males have a similar effect on humans. For some reason they are just naturally enthralled by our... well, beauty. Personally, I hate that part about me. I guess that's why I'm letting myself be a bit more at ease around you. You don't seem to be reacting to it like every other human male that I have known."

"Yeah, you're not the first to point that out." I answered, thinking back to Nisa. "From what I have been told, certain, natural magic and fae abilities don't have the usual effects on me. It used to anger a lot of the fae that tried to kill me over the years."

As we cleared the exit of the store we were immediately surrounded by a group of people all wearing shirts the read B. O. A. The way the all moved wasn't immediately threatening, but it was definitely off putting. Dawn immediately froze up, clearly no ok with the sudden attention that we were now getting. On that note, I was curious how this lot was able to perceive me with my hat and coat on.

"Excuse us you two," the lady closest to me said as she stepped toward us, "hello, my name is Janet and I represent Bethlehem's Outreach Association and I was wondering if you two had a moment to talk to us."

"Um, we were kind of busy." I answered, not sure how to go about this interaction.

"Oh this won't take long." Janet answered cheerfully. "We just want to know if you two have accepted Jesus Christ as your savior? He died for our sins so that we can be forgiven and accepted into the paradise of Heaven."

"Oh shit…" I sighed in relief and annoyance. "Listen, I have it on good authority that Christ doesn't back the majority of the churches and groups that carry out crap in his name. And personally, the two of us have had all of the religion that we can handle in several lifetimes. So, if you can just let us through, we will be on our merry and you can go about saving the souls of other hapless dopes who you manage to corner."

I grabbed Dawn by the wrist gently and tried to push past Janet and her posse of churchy do-gooders. Apparently this sent the wrong signal to Janet, because instead of moving out of my way, her and her lackeys actually cut us off and barred our way further. The lot of them was now gathered in front of us, still smiling. But I no longer viewed them as non-threatening. This was Westboro Baptist Church level behavior, and I knew Dawn was not ready for this so soon after her captivity.

"Listen Karen," I began as I stepped back and pulled Dawn behind me, "I don't know what you're selling here, but we're not buying. So why don't you back up and let me get my friend home."

"Actually my name is Janet, but that's ok." Janet corrected with a fake laugh. "Is your friend ok? You know, we can pray for her. It is only through God's light that we are healed of our burdens."

"Like I said," I snapped, "we will pass! Now move."

But they didn't move. They all joined Janet's hands and began praying, loudly for the health and well being of their newfound, poor and unfortunate friends. We were trapped between a one way opening automatic door and a wall of people who clearly were more than what they seemed and they were praying for us. My pulse began to race as my anger grew. Something inside me was screaming for me to just shoot them now and be done with it, but I knew that I couldn't where Dawn and I were. Yet, the longer they prayed, the more I struggled with telling myself no. As I felt my hand moving to my hip, they prayer ceased.

"I would like to invite the two of you to a metal music festival that Bethlehem is hosting." Janet said as she reached beneath a clipboard that she was holding and pulled out two tickets. "This even is by invite only, and I think that you two would greatly benefit from being there."

"Yeah, fine, whatever." I barked. "If I take the tickets will you leave us the hell alone?!"

"Oh don't be so negative." Janet laughed in her faux falsetto tone again. "The date of the festival is on the tickets, I hope to see you both in attendance. If you do show, I can promise you that I can personally get you to meet the bands backstage."

"Ok, sure." I said as I snatched the tickets from her now outstretched hand.

The moment we had those tickets in my possessions, the group parted and let us through. I didn't wait for them to change their minds, as I scooped Dawn up the same way I did the night we had met and carried her to my car. I got her into the passenger seat and jumped behind the steering wheel a half a moment later. I cranked the keys over to start the engine and took off out of that parking lot like a bat out of Hell down a road that ran parallel along the West side of Highway 273.

While we drove in silence, I saw a sign for a bookstore and I took a sharp turn into the parking lot beneath the sign, hoping to find a quiet place to regain our bearings. I drove to the back of the parking lot until there was only the building to my left and a chain link fence in front of me. I glanced over at the structure and spotted a little hole-in-the-wall bookstore. I parked my car in the spaces across from the entrance and just stopped.

Silence settled between Dawn and myself, the only sounds were the soft exhales of her breathing out and the heavy sounds of my quickened, respiratory heaving. Finally, it was her who broke the heavy hush that was steadily blanketing the two of us heavily.

"What the hell was that?!" She practically screamed.

"I don't know." It wasn't normal, that's for sure."

"Ya think?!" She snapped, clearly terrified. Tears began rushing down her cheeks as she sobbed between breaths. "Every one of my senses told me that they were dangerous, but I froze. I couldn't do anything. I was paralyzed and I couldn't do a damn thing!"

"It's ok Dawn." I tried to console her. "I was there and I got us through it. Your instincts were right. They were able to notice me through the magical wards on my hat and coat. That's not normal. It takes either practice or someone who is gifted with magic themselves to be able to do that."

"That doesn't make it any better." Dawn shouted. "What the hell is wrong with me?! I should have been able to fight them off or run, but instead I seized up and froze in place."

"This was your first adventure out into the world again after being held a prisoner for years on in." I told her sternly. "You probably have PTSD from everything that you went through. It's a small wonder that you are able to function as well as you have. You are stronger than anyone that I have met in a long time. And that's the truth."

Dawn stifled a whimper as she nodded and wiped her eyes. I gave her a few minutes to get herself together. All I could think of was how weird it was that those Jesus-freaks were able to see me. And not just that woman Janet. Something told me that all of them were well aware of my presence and didn't even notice the magical wards emanating from my hat or coat.

"Where are we." Dawn asked suddenly.

"A used book store I saw." I answered meekly. "I figured we needed someplace quiet to regain our composure before venturing out again, and I have always loved the smell of used books. I figured that this was as good as place as any."

"Goddess, you're such a nerd!" Dawn laughed. "But books and quiet are good things. Lead on hero."

"I thought that I told you that I'm not a hero." I replied.

"Says the man who has saved my ass two times now." Dawn answered with a wry smile. "Oh and didn't you mention that you've saved the world twice in total."

"So what?" I answered defensively. "I'm still not a hero."

"Do you know what the definition of a hero is?" Dawn asked in return. "Someone who gets other people killed."

"Holy crap!" I bleated excitedly. "You quoted Serenity! Who is the nerd now?!"

"Clearly you." Dawn answered.

We both laughed, finally at ease and somewhat past the incident that transpired just minutes before. I felt my phone vibrate, and I pulled it out to investigate. It was a text from Rook, which was out of character for him because he hated texting.

"We have a PROBLEM!"

"Oh balls, what now?!" I spat.

CHAPTER 9
WASTE NOT, WANT NOT

Zachariah made sure that he never wasted a drop. Even when others would say that his glass was drained, he would patiently wait until every drop of dear fluid danced across his palette and down his throat. Life was too precious to waste and as such, so were its offerings. There were those amongst the Elders that were greedy yet wasteful, letting such valuable nectar pool in miniscule gatherings, settled at the bottoms of their cups. But not he. Zachariah knew that every drop wasted was a moment of life wasted, and he was determined to savor every minute that he imbibed.

The banqueted hall was empty now. The officers and the other Elder's had left Zachariah to his drink, never sticking around to finish their own sacred beverages. Their cups and glasses were littered across the tables, set down to be cleaned up by some lesser member of their organization; hoping to one day join them in a moment such as the one that had just happened. The help knew better to enter the Banquet Hall until Zachariah had left. They dared not sully the ritual nor his quiet and patient final seconds of partaking.

Zachariah reflected on today's bouquet. He imagined what it must be like to be so young yet be so sequestered from life itself. To have the potential for so much, yet to squander it on decrepit hobbies such as video gaming. He wondered what would possess someone to pursue such a lifestyle when such a beautiful world was out their ready to be explored and enjoyed. If one wanted an escape into fantasy, there were so many wonderful books that could garner such a flight from reality. But to devote any and all free time to staying indoors and staring at a screen was so… distastefully lavish. It was truly a waste of one's life. But surely now, the remaining years of youth would not be frittered away. Those years would be put to good use, for betterment of Bethlehem.

Zachariah smiled as he felt the last trickle of moisture from his glass dance playfully down his throat. He set his cup down gingerly, looking into its mouth one final time to inspect its final contents. It was truly empty, giving him a sense of propriety and accomplishment as he looked again at his fellows cups. He fought back a noise of disgust as he reviled in their wanton waste. If were less-enlightened, Zachariah would have been tempted to finish draining each vestibule such valuable ambrosia.

If. But, he was not and Zachariah never took more than his fair share. If the others chose to not finish theirs, it was their loss. Let it be a reward for those who cleaned up. Their faith should be rewarded somehow. Why not give them what would otherwise be washed down a drain in the kitchens. It was he who had brought this suggestion to the Elders and officers, and they all absently agreed. They didn't see their actions as wasteful. So they didn't care if the help licked their dishes clean. As long as they received their fill first.

And so it had been for the last two years as their organization traveled the world. With every new city, there were new vintages to enjoy for everyone. Redding was no different. And with this first tasting, Zachariah knew there were many more years of life to save from those who would squander them otherwise amongst the citizens. Bethlehem accepted anyone from any clique, social class, or walks of life. They were all welcome to the table. Once they came to Bethlehem, their remaining years of life would never be misused or wasted again.

Zachariah exited the Banquet Hall and gave the nod of approval for the cleaning crew to enter. He did not look back to inspect their work. They all knew the price of failure in their tasks. Failure was a waste of time. A waste of time, was a waste of life. And that was simply not tolerated within Bethlehem ranks, less they find themselves committing their lives to the organization indefinitely.

Such thoughts were undesirable and unpalatable after such a fine cask and were better left in the dark of the hall with the help and the remains of the banquet itself. Zachariah started humming a tune as he made his way down the hallway to the building's main foyer.

Being the public face of Bethlehem, Zachariah had multiple meetings to attend to. The City Council demanded his immediate attention. He needed to make sure the proper people were met, and all of the correct I's were dotted and T's were crossed before they began planning further for their event. They preferred anonymity and control of any events that they held and sometimes, that require special approaches in certain cities.

Redding probably was no different. With the right amount of posturing, promises, and profits given to the right individuals, Zachariah knew that Bethlehem could do whatever the hell that they wanted. Experience had taught him that almost everyone in power wanted more power, and those that didn't could be moved. Yet, from what he had gleaned from his previous interactions with this city, he suspected he would find little resistance.

Resistance was a waste of time. Time was life, and Zachariah hated any wasted moments of life more than anyone else. Each moment wasted was a drop of blood falling from one's body, like grains of sand falling through an hour glass. And like he had said before, Zachariah never wasted a drop.

CHAPTER 10
KEEPING THE WORD

The clattering of old, brass bells greeted Dawn and I as we entered the old book store. The immediate aroma of ancient tomes and volumes delightfully greeted my senses as my eyes took in the main entry of the shop. Shelves reaching the ceiling climbed the walls on both sides of us, full to the brim with a mass collection of knowledge and stories from over the ages. In the corner to the left of the door was a massive crystal cluster, slightly dusty, but still beautiful in its natural form.

In the center of this room sat four glass display cases acting as an enclosed counter space. On top of the half on the left was a stack of various paperbacks and hard-covers, all awaiting to find a home among the hoard of written words that surrounded us. The display case facing the door contained various, old and clearly rare titles, proudly displayed for everyone to see. A basic cash register sat somewhere behind, clearly on a small table within the enclosed space. I could see openings to other parts of the building on either side of the displays, leading into the stacks of books hidden within.

And near the register within the four displays, stood the shopkeeper. He was a short man, with a solidly upright posture. His short hair was showing signs of aging, but still held a perfect blend of color and graying. He had heavy brows and piercing eyes behind a pair of wire-frame spectacles. All of that paired with his tight-lipped smile that seemed to rest naturally on his expression, gave the man a striking resemblance of an intimidating old owl guarding his library.

"Welcome." The shopkeeper said as he waved at us. He gave us a quick smile in greeting, silently taking in our appearance, well mine more than Dawn's. He returned his attention to what he had been doing before he entered and gesture with his hand to his right. "Adult fantasy and science fiction is over that way."

"Thanks," I said looking at Dawn as if offended.

Clearly she was fighting back a giggle, obviously amused how the shopkeeper had read me as easily as a children's book. I guess I should feel grateful that he hadn't suggested we go to that section. I walked silently past him to the area he had recommended, continuing to take in the sheer mass of texts that this store had accumulated within its walls. It was impressive to say the least. We made our way through the opening and began found a room with even more floor to ceiling shelves. I took and immediate right and began meandering among the shelves.

I wasn't sure how long I had been at before I turned a noticed Dawn staring at me. Her face was almost void of all signs of emotion, which was a bit terrifying. I let my hand drift away from the spine of a title I had been looking at and turned to her.

"What's on your mind?" I asked.

"What are we doing?" Dawn answered.

"What do you mean?" I inquire. "I told you, we needed someplace quiet to center ourselves after those weirdoes put a whammy on us."

"I know that," Dawn shrilled quietly. "But you looked at what you have assured me is your cell phone before coming in here and wasn't happy. What, aren't you telling me?"

"I don't know myself." I answered honestly. "I just received a message from Rook saying that we have a problem. I'm not sure what that is, but if he isn't texting me or calling me, that means he can't. He'll show up soon enough and give us the details when he can. Until that time, there's nothing that we can do, except recoup ourselves like I suggested."

"I don't get you Danny?" Dawn answered looking down. "You have been through so much, have had so many horrible things happen to you and those you care about, and you just keep on soldiering through it. How do you do it? How do you look into that abyss and not fall into it?"

"Well the thing is, the longer that you stare out into the abyss…" I paused as I inhaled deeply, "eventually the abyss gets annoyed and tells you to take a damn picture so the moment lasts. Then you realize that you've lost your shit because you are talking to and reply for existential existence."

I paused a moment and tried to see Dawn's expression. Her eyes were locked on the floor still. After a second or so, she lifted her chin slightly, glancing up to me. I gave her a brief smirk and exhaled loudly.

"So I don't stare into the abyss, I get drunk and piss into it." I said, trying to break the somber ambiance that had settled heavily over the conversation. "In all reality, it's best not to think about this crap at all. It makes it easier to do what I do that way."

That earned a genuine chuckle from Dawn as she began scanning the titles on the shelves in front of her.

"How did I fall in with such a nerd?" She asked as she pulled a random book down. She held it aloft for me to see, displaying a clearly overly-fantasized elf on the cover. "Why does every writer have the impression that we are all glowing and sparkly and magical?"

"I couldn't tell you." I answered. "I like Brooks' and Tolkien's elves. They're magical yes, but they are nitty-gritty and have flaws. And that's what makes something relatable. Not perfection, but flaws."

"Well Tolkien still put elves on too high of a pedestal." Dawn answered, sliding the book back on the shelf. "I haven't read anything of Brooks, so I can't really give much credence to his portrayal of elves."

"Well, I have a few of his books, I'll let you peruse them if you want to." I answered. "And is that another reason why the other fae rejected the elves?"

"From what I know, yes." Dawn answered dryly. "The elves just weren't the perfectionists that the rest of the fair folk were. Sure, in terms of magical ability, we were as skilled as many of the highborn fae, yet we never held to their ideals and their emotionless dribble and their word games. So they rejected elves causing the entirety of the species to live on this side of the Veil."

"Yeah," I answered, "after spending as much time with them as I have, I have no patience for their crap either."

"The fae can burn for all I care." Dawn seethed. "When elves were being hunted down and murdered by the humans, they turned their backs on us for such petty reasons."

The noise of the front doors opening interrupted anything that I might have said. A quiet hush fell between Dawn and I, which was short lived, because the high falsetto of a eerily familiar voice greeting the shopkeeper wafted in, muffled by the multitude of books. I heard no footsteps following, only an intense pressure of a threat suddenly looming nearby.

"Sir, if I may, you have the most quaint store that I have ever seen." The voice chimed cheerfully.

"My store has been around for a long time." The shopkeep replied curtly.

"Well having solid roots is something to be proud of." The voice answered.

I poked my head around the corner and spotted the same group of do-gooders whom had assailed Dawn and I standing in the doorway. They held the door ajar, but had yet to enter through its opening. They stood their staring inside with their empty smiles and eyes that seemed to only mirror what they saw, yet were soulless and hollow, I had been so caught up in the panic of the moment from our last encounter that I hadn't had the notion to take in these details. And then it clicked…

"They are not real." I whispered shrilly.

"Quiet!" Hissed Dawn. She motioned for me to come back. "What do you mean that they're not real?!"

"I think those bible thumpers are magical constructs." I answered. "And I think that there is more to this book store than meets the eye. I should have guessed as much when we entered. A crystal that big by the main entrance isn't just for ambiance."

"You're right..." Dawn added as she peeked around the corner. "They're not coming inside at all."

"Exactly..." I said. I held my finger to my lips to silence the conversation for the time being as I waited for the shopkeeper's response.

"Yes, it is." The owlish man answered with an impatient sigh. The same sigh that you hear an elder make when they are done playing games with whichever youthful idiocy is causing them to waste their time and patience.

"Oh yes!" the woman exclaimed from the door way. Her hand slipped into her shoulder bag and emerged with a stack of papers almost immediately after. "We noticed that you had flyers in your window advertising for various musicians and what not and I was wondering if you would be willing to hang flyers for my organization's concert event. We're called Bethlehem and we have multiple outreach programs for the poverish and underprivileged communities."

"That is so… seemingly nice of you." The shopkeep answered, clearing taking time to choose his words carefully. It was almost fae-like. "But I think that I will have to decline. I allow LOCAL artists and musicians to advertise through my windows as I support the arts. I have little use for organizations, churches, or cults."

"But sir, we support the local community." The woman answered, her voice never wavering in her fake cheer.

"You have my answer." The shopkeeper replied, as he returned to whatever he had been doing before they had interrupted him.

The leader Janet seemed to almost twitch at his refusal but never broke her composure. She simply set the stack of flyers in the door way and turned away. I didn't see if they group got into a vehicle, and I didn't care. I was beginning to have some serious worries about this Bethlehem. They had magical lackies out performing prayer circles. It definitely didn't sit right with me.

I attempted to turn to Dawn, only to find her peering over my shoulder. I nearly fell to keep from bowling her over in my movement to turn around. After a few awkward twists and grasps for balance, we managed to regain composure.

"That was enlightening." Dawn said.

"No kidding." I replied. "I'm not sure what they are, but Janet and her prayer posse are clearly not human. They're some sort of magical construct. I just don't know which kind."

"It's best to leave those types of mysteries unsolved. The shopkeeper answered from behind his counter. "If one of you would be kind enough to fetch those flyer for me, I would appreciate it. I have my hands full."

We walked out to find the shopkeeper placing a protective covering around a dust jacket very carefully. He seemed wholly focused on his task and never lifted his eyes to us. I walked to the door and picked up the papers. It was a stack of flyers advertising the very event that they had insisted that Dawn and I attend earlier. I glared at them as I returned to the counter.

"Hand them here so that I can file them." The shopkeeper instructed as he held one hand out and inspected his work held in his other.

I passed the papers to him and without breaking concentration he dumped them unceremoniously into a blue recycling bin behind him. His free hand returned to the book, which he now held in front of him. He set it down gently and placed his hands on the counter and leaned forward, resting his weight on them.

"Now, were you two here looking for something particular or were you hiding from those things." He asked gruffly.

"Sorry," I answered with a pitiful smile. "We actually had come in here to look, but we had run into them before we came here, so we weren't too keen to interact with them again."

"Well Mr. Nimbus, you and your elf friend here seem to have gotten mixed up with something entirely nasty." The shopkeeper answered as he grabbed the book and put in on top of a growing stack behind him.

I instinctively reached for my gun as he spoke. Not many knew me as Danny Nimbus. He also seemed to know that Dawn was an elf. I stepped away from the counter and placed myself between Dawn and him.

"Oh good grief!" he responded without looking at me. "Drop the macho, fae boogeyman façade. I'm too old to deal with such ignorant masculine displays of testosterone."

"Who are you?!" I spat. "What are you?!"

"I am old." He answered. "I am a keeper of books. The written word is my ward to protect. And I have… for so very long."

"Who are you?" Dawn asked again for me.

"I am the proprietor of this book store and time is money here." He replied with a grim, tight-lipped smile. Again, I was reminded of an impatient old owl. "You need not worry. I know who you are boy, and I have no intention of acting on that knowledge. And I could sense that your friend was an elf the moment she entered. Again, be at ease. It is a crime that so few of her kind are left. I would never act to further that fact."

"Oh," I answered after a minute of heavy silence. "I guess we will get out of your hair then."

Dawn and I turned to leave. As we neared the door, I felt the presence of the shopkeep behind us. I heard him clear his throat to get our attention. Dawn yelped and I jumped in unison. We spun to face him, not sure what to expect. He held out a green, double pointed stone spire. Darker swirls of green danced across its polished surface. He approached Dawn slowly, holding the stone aloft in his hand. He waited for her to respond to his approach. She carefully opened her hands, clearly not sure how respond to this random stranger offering her something.

"Take this." The shopkeeper instructed, his voice no longer impatient and surly. "It will help protect you as long as you carry it on you."

He dropped the stone into her open hands. Her grip closed around it immediately, as her life depended on her taking this random stone. I looked to him, and found a soft smile. Before I could comment though, he turned and walked away. I looked to Dawn, now clutching the stone to her chest. A look somewhere between panic and relief raced to and fro across her face. I pushed the door open, holding it aloft for Dawn to exit first. As she stepped out I felt the presence of the shopkeeper again, but this time he was nowhere near me. I just knew that he had his attention now focused on me and it was almost unbearable.

"You would be wise to let her go." I heard him say inside my mind. "Keeping her in your life will only lead to pain."

"I will protect her better than your stone." I answered irritably out loud. Dawn turned and gave me a confused look.

"So be it." His voice sighed.

As I felt his presence lift, I was left with a feeling of sadness. Not mine, but his. It was a sadness that I was accustomed to, but much older and much deeper. It was almost unbearable. But I did what I have always done. I gave Dawn a smile that probably made me look ridiculous, and I continued forward. We reached the car, and as Dawn entered from the passenger side, I hesitated and looked back at the store front. I couldn't feel anything anymore. I stared, until I knew that there was nothing left of the shopkeeper with me. Nothing but his words.

CHAPTER 11
COFFEE & KRYPTONITE

As Dawn and I pulled into the drive, we found a very flustered Rook waiting for us. His rotund face was flushed, either from the heat, anger, or quite possibly both. Regardless of which option it was, I could tell that he wasn't in a good mood. As soon as the Gremlin ceased moving, Rook was moving towards us. I had barely gotten my door open before his large frame was there, iron-gripping my door from the opposite side.

"Where the hell have you been?!" Rook snapped. "I get back here and find you both gone. All I found was the closet ransacked and dresses thrown everywhere."

"Whoa there," I said as I got out, "dial it back a notch, Pops. We just went to get Dawn some clothes that suited her better. Besides, since when have you been so keen on my private life?"

"Since today!" Rook shouted. "Didn't you get my text?!"

"Take it easy, Dad!" Dawn mocked. "He got that text a while ago, but we were already out and about."

"Ok, no offense, but I don't even know you." Rook barked, waving a manila file folder between us. "And this is serious. I have a case in the area, and eventually the FBI will be sending me some extra help to work this case. And if they see you, I won't be able to play stupid and let you go."

"What case could they possibly want to put you on?!" I asked sourly as Rook slapped the folder into my chest.

I thumbed the file open and let my eyes scan the front page. I wasn't planning on seriously giving this thing a proper read until I read the Suspect's name, Bethlehem. The moment my gaze fell on that name my whole body froze. Every memory from today came flooding back to me concerning Janet and her flunkey patrol.

"Holy shit…" I whispered. "Crap, crap, crap, crap, crap!"

"Danny what is it?" Dawn asked, worry cracking behind her words.

"Yeah, seriously kid," Rook added, "care to share with the rest of us?!"

"You're investigating Bethlehem." I replied, flicking the folder closed. "We ran into some of their… do-gooders earlier today. And I can tell you that they weren't human."

"What were they?" Rook asked, switching his tone to his cop mode. "Fae, undead, daemons, what are we dealing with?"

"They weren't any of those." I answered. "From what I could tell, they were some sort of magical constructs."

"What the hell is a magical construct?!" Rook snapped.

"Well, it is an artificial creature made from magic." I answered. "Golems and homunculi are examples of magical constructs."

"Golems?" Rook inquired incredulously. "Like made from clay or stone?"

"Or flesh." I added. "Remember that thing we killed before we met Azrael? That's a type of magical construct."

"You mean that thing that I smashed the pistachio on its head?" Rook asked.

"Yup!" I answered. "I just don't know exactly what kind they are.

"Wait, did I just hear that right?" Dawn chimed in. "You killed a flesh golem with a pistachio?"

"Yes, we did." I answered idly.

"How does that even make any sense?!" Dawn exclaimed.

"It had been animated by Voo Doo." I replied.

"Oh, well that just clears everything up." Dawn answered snidely.

"Welcome to my world." Rook sighed as he let go of the car and took the file back from me. "Let's get inside and figure out our next steps. I'll put some coffee on."

"Great! I need some right about now." I added as I swung my legs out and followed Rook towards the castle.

"Isn't anyone going to help me carry my stuff in?" Dawn called to us.

"Nah," I answered, "You're a strong, independent woman. You've got this."

I heard Rook stifle a laugh. I could see him shake his head and I wondered what was going through his mind at that moment. I ran and caught up with him; then gave him an inquisitive look.

"You're so naïve with women." He chuckled. "She is going to put you through the wringer now, and I am going to stand back and watch."

"What?!" I asked.

"Let me put this in terms that you can grasp." Rook laughed. "I just found your Kryptonite."

"You mean aside from the hail of bullets, spells, and bladed weaponry that I have had used against me in the past?" I replied.

"Oh no, that stuff could kill you." Rook chortled. "But it wasn't your Kryptonite. That girl back there… oh she has her hooks in you and you are too stupid to see it."

"Wait, are you saying that Dawn is my Kryptonite?" I spat. "Dude, it's not like that… we're not like that…"

"Ok, tell yourself whatever you need to." Rook laughed again. "Just remember, in the end, be careful. Don't get hurt and try not to get too attached."

"You're giving me dating advice?" I snapped.

"Yes, I am!" Rook snapped back. "The closest thing that you have had to a healthy relationship was a near death encounter with a succubus. But we're digressing from my original point."

"Which was…?"

"I'm happy that you're happy right now." Rook replied. "But she knows that you've got the hots for her and you just brushed her off… Kryptonite."

"Crap…" I muttered. "Kryptonite."

I turned to see if Dawn was managing ok. She was. However, if looks could kill, I would have keeled over. Her expression was almost stoic… almost. However, I noted that Dawn was clearly pursing her lips a little too tightly together and her eyes were just slightly narrowed. I took a deep breath, turned around, and made my way back to her.

"Let me help you with those." I offered.

"Nope," Dawn answered neutrally. "I got them."

She shoved past me and made her way towards the castle. On her way past Rook, he turned to me and gave me a gritted-teeth smile. He shook his head again and followed behind Dawn. I could almost hear his chuckling in my head. I took a deep breath and hurried to catch up.

I knew that I had more important things to worry about, but a part of me was screaming at myself for slighting Dawn. I wasn't sure how, but I made a promise to myself to get back into her good graces somehow. I just couldn't figure out why it mattered so much to me?

"One problem at a time." I said to myself.

Apparently I had other problems to deal with, and they were called Bethlehem. Again, I let the feelings from the day's encounters flood through me in hopes to give me focus. Yet, I was unable to stop a stray thought from invading my concentration before following Dawn and Rook into the castle.

"Kryptonite, damn you!" I whispered to myself.

CHAPTER 12
IDLE HANDS

At this point I had read Rook's case file three times and it still made my stomach churn. Their movements and behavior painted a clear picture of what was going on behind the scenes, especially after I had a run in with the things that they sent out on their behalf. Janet and the other constructs had me worried now more than ever. Their behavior at the book store was definitely worrisome, but now it was in a whole new cadre of troubling.

I tossed the folder onto the table in front of me and raked my hands through my hair in frustration. Rook had left to find a motel and left the file with me to familiarize myself with before he returned. It was so eerily quiet I could hear my own veins pumping blood. Or at least it felt that way. It was because of this, that the sudden sound of Dawn grabbing the folder and dragging it across the table caused me to jump in alarm.

Ok, let me be honest, I fell over backwards in my chair trying to get away while reaching for my sidearm. Overall, I failed on all counts and was unceremoniously ejected onto my back. It was not a flattering scene.

The sounds of Dawn giggling laughter rang in the air as I made my attempt to stand up without making myself look like an idiot any further.

"Easy there." Dawn chortled as she gingerly lifted the file from the table and flicked it open. "You're a jumpy one."

"Yeah… force of habit in my line of work." I attempted to laugh feebly.

"Well, relax." Dawn scolded. "I'm not trying to kill you."

"Yeah, yeah…" I guffed as I stood my chair up and sat back down. "The contents of the case are a bit of a doozy. It paints a pretty horrible picture coupled with the experiences that we have had with them today."

"I can see that." Dawn answered blankly. "Now shut up and let me read."

I closed my mouth and ended any further attempt at a conversation. I knew that she would engage me when she was done, given what she was reading, but I was unsure how the conversation would pan out. I waited silently, trying to keep myself as relaxed as possible, but I was unable to manage to do so.

I felt my body shift beneath me. I heard every creak of these wooden chairs and I groaned internally, hoping that I didn't anger Dawn further than I had already achieved earlier. After a few agonizingly infinite minutes crawling by, she set the folder down and looked up at me.

"So, are you guys going to shut Bethlehem down?" Dawn asked as she slid the folder back to me.

"That's the plan, I think." I replied, catching the folder with my finger tips. "We'll discuss it further when Rook gets back. But, we're definitely going to want to end this before anymore FBI get into the area. I kind of like where I've been laying low lately. And I really don't want to go back to being on the run."

"Yeah, that sounds pretty crappy." Dawn mused absently. "But back to the matter at hand. I want in."

"What?!" I snorted.

"I want to help you guys take down Bethlehem." She answered. "Three people are better than two, and I have a few skills where magic is concerned."

"What about what happened earlier today." I asked. I knew my worry screamed behind my words. "If that happens while we're out working, it could get us into some deep crap."

"I should be fine." Dawn answered dismissively. "That just happened because they were suddenly surrounding us and I could feel that something was off about them. Now that I know, I will be prepared for it."

"I don't know…" I answered. "I don't want you to get hurt."

"Stop right there." Dawn snapped. "You're not my boyfriend or my caretaker. You don't get to act that way towards me. I can handle myself. I thought that I made that clear earlier today before we even left."

"Oh, ok. I got it…" I answered in defeat. I felt something sink in me emotionally. "I'll run it by Rook when he gets back. He should be ok with it."

Dawn nodded in agreement and I suddenly didn't know what to do with myself. I looked around the room and was saved by the sight of my work bench. I picked myself up from my chair and meandered over to it. I let my subconscious mind take over, as I began dismantling my gun and cleaning it. When I was done and it was reassembled, I turned to my smelting kit and turned it on. I let instinct direct my hands as I began the process of making shotgun shells that could be used to combat the supernatural. It was busy work, but something that I easily absorbed myself into.

I lost myself into the process of melting gold and silver down into pellets first, creating the innards for my ammunitions. After I hat filled enough shell, I moved on to melting down the remaining precious metals into ingots for selling. I didn't fund myself with UNICEF and supplies were needed.

"What are you doing?" I heard Dawn ask from over my shoulder.

"Making ammo that I can use to kill the various species of fae, undead, and other supernatural things that like to try and kill me when I work." I answered mechanically as I moved to loading a shotgun shell with small diamonds.

I rarely used rounds like these, mainly because they were so damn expensive to make. Not to mention that the list of creatures that they were effective against was pretty small. But ever since I had run into a wraith and found out that they were immune to pretty much everything I realized it was wise to have at least a few around for good measure.

"How do you know what works against what?" Dawn inquire curiously.

"I asked the Queen of the Seelie Court for information." I replied absently. "Besides that, trial and error after reading many old legends from around the world. If you are curious, I have outlined a lot of it in my journals which are on the shelf next to my bench here."

"Maybe I will." Dawn answered. "So the Queen just gave you this information, out of the kindness of her heart?!"

"Hell no!" I barked a laugh. "Kindness had nothing to do with it. She was at war and I was a weapon. And I was most effective if I was well informed. I'd bet a silver quarter that she probably wants to dispose of me with how much I know."

"Then why hasn't she?" Dawn asked.

"Because she can't." I replied. "I've still got the backing of an arch angel and she doesn't want to piss of a divine being. As queen, she only plays at being divine. Azrael on the other hand was the Angel of Death. She doesn't quite have the juice to throw down with him. Not to mention that I am fairly sure that I owe Lucifer a favor; and magical favors are pretty hard to navigate around when attempting to off someone who is bound by them."

"You're in this pretty deep then?" Dawn answered more than asked.

"Have been since the beginning." I snapped as I finished pouring molten gold into an ingot mold. "I really didn't have a choice in the matter. I was drug into this life under the threat of death and that never really changed."

I heard Dawn moving to my left, and I caught a glimpse of her picking up one of my various journals and flicking through it. She would stop every other page and skim the contents, sometimes stopping longer to read the entire section. I left her to it and returned my attention to my bench.

I finished what I was working on, removed my gloves, and scooped the ammunition up. I turned and made my way to where I kept to storage cases for ammo. I deposited the shells in their respective containers. I meant to return my attention towards my work station, but instead let my gaze settle on Dawn. I jerked myself away, muttering to myself as I made my way to the kitchen.

"Damn it Rook, where are you?!" I growled at myself. "Fucking Kryptonite."

"Did you say something?" Dawn called from the main study where I had set up my possessions when I moved in. "It sounded like you said Kryptonite."

"Yeah, I was just talking to myself." I called back.

"Nerd!" Dawn teased loudly.

I turned away from her voice, more irritated with myself, than her. Suddenly I felt her presence behind me as her chin came to rest gently on my shoulder. She draped one of her arms on my shoulder and coiled the other around my stomach.

"Well, I guess you're also a bit of a badass." Dawn sighed contently. "But you're still a nerd."

"Thanks…" I croaked, as I tried not to gasp in relief. I felt my whole body flush as she rested against me. "Hey, sorry for my commentary in the driveway. I may have meant in as a joke, but it was tactless."

"Don't worry about it." Dawn laughed. "I decided to let it go."

"Since when?" I asked.

"Since I finished reading your journal." Dawn. I felt her lean forward and bite my ear lobe playfully. "Now, what do you have to eat here? I'm famished!"

She released her arms from me and I could feel her energy untangle from my own. It was a horrible and amazing sensation all at once and it left me wanting more. I fought that feeling down and made my way to fridge. I opened the door dramatically, revealing its contents to Dawn.

"That all depends on what you're in the mood for." I answered.

"How about you make us some sandwiches and we go upstairs." Dawn teased, sending a shiver down my spine.

"Sounds good." I stammered in reply.

I watched her leave the room and make her way to the stairs. She paused in the doorway to the kitchen and gave me a mischievous wink, and then disappeared towards the stairs. I leaned forward and banged my head against the freezer door.

"Kryptonite, damn you!" I groaned. I knew that it wouldn't be the last time.

CHAPTER 13
WORK RELATED EXPIRATION

After several phone calls, Rook had managed to locate the current office for Bethlehem in the Redding City limits. For such a public company, it had beyond difficult to find their building of operations. This in itself was a huge red flag as far as Rook was concerned. And now he was on his way to the proverbial lion's den. He was hoping that his sudden appearance would stagger someone within their fold and rustle a lead loose. He hoped.

Currently Rook had stopped at a gas station near a heavily urban retail area, which just so happened to be around the corner from Bethlehem's office. Rook wasn't sure what was going to happen when he showed up, but he would rather not take the chance of running out of gas after kicking this particular hornet's nest.

In his brief time in the area, he had come to notice that the city of Redding had a heavy homeless population and that it seemed to getting worse. Hell, just today he had lost count how many he had seen with signs and asking for handouts. This made the city a prime location for Bethlehem's shady practices.

And no sooner as he noted that he was being watched by a particularly loathsome and unkempt figure in the brush and bramble along the slope of greenery alongside the freeway that ran parallel with this gas station. He noted that there was a hole in the fence that separated the gas station from the freeway, clearly an easement for the transients that dwelled among the shrubbery.

The gas pump clicked and he replaced the nozzle, never breaking his peripheral vision from the apparent homeless person eyeing him. Rook got in his car and parked it in the side parking area next to the main store building. He reached over and grabbed his backup firearm, remembering that it still had iron rounds in it. He slipped it in his main holster on his hip and exited the vehicle. He scanned the fence-line and easily found the mark he was looking for.

Upon closer inspection, he noted that his mark had vaguely female features. Yet, either she had fallen into a vat of acid and never had healed from the blisters, or she was on some new street drug that aged her horribly and damaged her skin. Aside from the grotesque abscesses or wart like blisters, her skin was graying with rot in some areas and sagging horribly in other areas. Her wardrobe was rag-like and slightly oversized.

"Hello… mamm'," Rook addressed her as he cautiously approached. "I couldn't help but notice you keeping watch over me as I pumped my gas. I'd like to inquire why?"

"Oh he addresses us as if we're equal." The woman croaked and cackled. "He wants to know why we watched him. Why indeed? Tell me, what do you know about the area?"

"Not much, I'm afraid." Rook answered honestly.

"Tis' dangerous, always dangerous." The woman chortled sinisterly. "We watch because we see everything."

"Do you now?" Rook asked, struggling to not sound intrigued. "Do you know of any possible people being abducted or going missing?"

"Perhaps, we do." The woman answered shrilly. "Why don't you come with us to our lair and we show you what we know."

"Is it on the other side of that fence?" Rook asked carefully.

"Yes, oh yes it is." The woman smiled wickedly. "Come now, come. You will learn that which we can divulge."

She didn't wait for his answer and simply disappeared through the hole in the fence. Every instinctual alarm that Rook had developed since meeting Danny was screaming at him that this was dangerous. But he needed answers and he knew that this woman knew something that he could use… be it in his case or to assist Danyael was still to be discovered. Rook pulled his sidearm from his hip and readied the hammer. He steadied the piece and ducked under the fence that the woman had vanished through only moments before.

As he pulled his leg through the last inch under the hole in the fence, the whole atmosphere changed. Rook was not in the open air next to the freeway anymore. Now he found himself in a poorly lit cement-like cave. The various smells of filth of rotten meat lashed out against his senses and caused him to almost wretch in response. But somehow, he managed to hold it together and not evacuate his stomach. He pulled out a small L.E.D. flashlight from his belt, clicking it on and shining blinding light into the surroundings. An eerie fog-like mist wafted along the ground, concealing everything from his knees down.

"The man actually followed us!" the woman's voice cackled from within the cave in front of him. "We're not sure if we want to hand this one over to the masters. We might want to birth an offspring with this one and feeds off him ourselves."

A shudder of sickening revulsion washed over Rook's entire being as his mind wrapped itself around the intent in her words. He steadied himself and then his gun and took a careful step into the cave.

"You said you could tell me about missing people?" Rook asked, trying to keep his mind alert. "Is it because of you?"

"Oh yes!" The woman cackled. "We are one of many. The masters have many servants to do their good work."

"So you take people for your masters or for yourself?" Rook asked as he slowly made his way step by step, deeper into towards this clear danger.

"Both." The woman laughed. "A girl has got to eat, after all. But that is only when the master has had their fill. But what the master does not know, will not hurt them."

"Then why tell me?" Rook asked worriedly.

"Because you will not be leaving here alive!" the woman bellowed in gleeful malevolence.

"Who are your masters then?" Rook asked. "Are they mages? Vampires? What type of monster holds your leash?"

"The masters are not monsters!" the woman's voice screeched in anger. "They are ascended from the very cattle that I feed upon. They are more, they are above, they are… beautiful."

"So they're human?" Rook asked, trying to keep this woman speaking so that he could locate her.

"No longer." The woman hissed from behind Rook. "You are food to them as you are to me."

Rook swallowed hard as he raised his gun to face the woman as he turned around. Accept, it was no longer a woman. What stood in front of him was a near seven foot tall monstrosity. It was les female in its appearance than it had been before. It wore tattered rags draped over random parts of its body and leaving parts that should be covered up, exposed. Its skin was more grey and putrid than before. The blisters and abscesses covered all of its skin, but in greater number. Its hair was matted, tangled and seemed to be wet.

"Oh he has a gun." The creature cackled. "He thinks his human weapon will harm me. Oh he does not know, he does not know!"

Rook opened fire and released a short, three burst round of shots into the thing's center mass. An outburst of screams of agony rang out from the creature as it fell backwards into the wall of the cave. The acrid scent of burning flesh sizzled in the humid air. One of its hands was held firm over its wound and the other was attempting to drag itself further away from Rook along the wall.

"I'm guessing by your reaction to those bullets that you are some sort of fae." Rook said as he kept his weapon trained on the thing in front of him.

"How does he know this?!" the creature gasped fearfully.

"And from what I can remember," Rook ignored her question and continued, "now that I have seen your real appearance, I am pretty sure that you are a hag."

Her eyes bulged in terror as Rook put a name to what she was. She struggled desperately to make her towering frame shrink and disappear. Her hand continued to scramble against the smooth wall, frantically searching for something that she could grab a hold of and pull herself to safety. She cupped her other hand over her wound, concealing the damage but not the smoke from the iron burning her flesh from inside her body.

"Now you are going to tell me what I need to know about your masters." Rook said, keeping his weapon pointed between her eyes. "If you cooperate, I might ease your suffering. Otherwise you are going to die very slowly from that wound and very painfully. Are we clear?!"

"Yes…" the Hag gurgled somewhere between terror and pain.

"Great!" Rook answered. "Now, are your masters the organization that goes by the name Bethlehem?"

"We cannot… we cannot speak of this!" the Hag whined.

"Why not?" Rook answered. "Do they have some spell on you that keeps you from speaking them?"

"No…" The Hag gasped. "We loves them. The masters loves us. They found us saved us. We would have died from The Order of Saint Patrick if not for the masters."

"You're going to die painfully right now if you don't tell me." Rook shouted. "Now tell me, hag! Are your masters the people who call themselves Bethlehem?!"

"We… Cannot… we… will not." The hag responded meekly.

Rook let his gun drift down slightly and shot her in each shoulder. The hag released a blood curdling scream as the iron bullets seared into her flesh. He wasn't sure if they had passed all the way through to the wall behind her, but Rook knew that it had been more painful than any normal G.S.W. to the shoulder.

"Do not make me keep asking." Rook demanded. "For your sake. Now, for the last time. Are your masters the human organization that calls themselves Bethlehem? I know that the fae cannot lie. But they can avoid the truth like you have been doing or bend it. Again, for your sake, I don't recommend either of those options."

"Masters are Bethlehem." The Hag sobbed in agony.

"See, was that so hard?" Rook asked, as he fired a last round into her forehead.

He let her body fall to the floor beneath the mist and turned and made his way back to where he came through at. He now knew that the FBI weren't going to be able to take care of Bethlehem. This was a job specifically suited to Danny Nimbus and Rook's complicated, secret life. He ducked under the fence, pulling his phone out to call Danny. This case was getting more and more complicated by the minute. Rook emerged into the parking lot of the gas station as if no time had passed at all. He furiously tapped MacClaude's number in and waited for him to pick up. As soon as Rook heard the line connect, he let loose.

"Alright, ass hole, this case just turned into a shit storm of hurricane proportions!" He shouted into the receiver. "I'm on my way back to you. I'll tell you all about it when I get there. Don't go anywhere."

Rook ended the call before MacClaude could answer. He reached his vehicle, unlocking it with the key fob as he approached. He tossed his phone in the seat and hauled himself behind the steering wheel. In a matter of seconds the engine was running and in gear as Rook tore out of the parking lot. It was at least a forty-five minute drive back to Danyael. Between then and now, hopefully Bethlehem didn't find their leashed monster in her lair. Hopefully they still had time to act. Hope was luxury and never an asset that Rook could count on. He pushed his foot down harder on his accelerator, propelling himself towards his destination at breakneck speeds.

CHAPTER FOURTEEN
A HOLE IN THE PLAN

I had arrived in town at the address that Rook had texted to me and was woefully underwhelmed. When I had received Rook's message it made me think that there was some major incident going down. But here he was, at a random gas station in Redding, at near dusk, where everyone could see them.

"You call me here for an emergency!" I hissed at Rook as I approached his SUV. "You are aware we are where everyone can see us?"

"Yes, I am!" Snapped Rook. "Just shut up and follow me."

Apparently, Dawn had gotten out of the Gremlin and followed behind me silently, so when I turned to motion for her to follow, I found her directly behind me. I jumped and let loose some very squeamish yelps and noises.

"Would you put a fricken' bell on or something!" I pleaded. "Yeesh, give a guy a heart attack…"

"Those sounds that you just made didn't inspire confidence in your manly capabilities." Dawn chuckled.

"Shut it." I snapped. "Let's go."

"Alright kiddos," Rook growled, "get the lead out or I will turn this car around and take you both home."

Dawn laughed, and I immediately relaxed. I felt my fear and tension lift, and suddenly being so exposed in public didn't matter so much. Rook had already walked away from Dawn and me; leaving us to follow after him. He eventually stopped in front of a chain-link fence that separated the gas station parking lot from the interstate that ran parallel behind the building. I noticed that there was a nice hole in the fence, large enough for a body to duck through. That in its self didn't seem too out of place. Especially in a city with such a high homeless population.

It was when Rook squatted down, moved through the hole, and then seemingly vanished that I decided that there might be a good reason for his emergency message after all. The obvious distortion of the air as his body clearly passed into a fae knowe made my stomach clench.

A knowe was essentially a pocket realm through the Veil where a fae had made a home for themselves. The best comparison that I had ever been able to find to describe how it worked, was comparing it to the TARDIS on Doctor Who. It was bigger on the inside. However it did have to technically adapt the realm that led to it. So if it was made in a forest, it would resemble the common concept of a fairy realm. But one made in a commercial area surrounded by asphalt, cement structures, and cars was something that I had never heard of before.

After a moment of hesitation, I gathered my resolve and ducked under the fence. My brain immediately protested the reality it was faced with as we stepped through a literal tear in the Veil and into this horrific knowe. I was disoriented and had barely staggered forward when Dawn came crashing through behind me. It wasn't just the sensation of passing through an unnatural breach within the very fabric of reality that made your mind reject that sensation and rebel against the vestibular coordination and balance that your body was saying that it experienced. It was the fact that you enter into this pocket realm in a crouching position and then suddenly, you're standing upright with no additional, physical motion taken by you.

The human brain can only filter so much. It has enough trouble trying to relay the existence of the magic of the Veil, without trying to correct the distortion in the laws of physics that your body goes through. Apparently the same was true with elves.

Dawn collided with my back as I heard her wretch upon passing through that opening. I could only guess that it was more horrid of an experience for her because of her ties to magic. I shuffled aside and gave her some space as she doubled over and placed her head between her knees. When I knew that she would be alright, I gave myself a moment to allow my head to stop swimming.

Rook, however, seemed completely un-phased by any of it. This made me completely irritated and highly envious. I took a shaky step forward, ignoring his puzzled and bemused gaze.

"What's wrong with you two?" Rook asked.

"You can't tell me that you didn't experience any of the negative feedback from passing through that tear in the Veil?!" I snapped bitterly.

"Nope." Rook assured. He gave me a look that I chose to interpret as smug and judgmental. "I have no clue what you're talking about. The only thing that I feel coming through there is uncomfortable and a bit flushed."

"Lucky you!" Dawn called to him.

"Apparently…" Rook trailed.

"So this is what you wanted to show us?" I asked, trying to move this along before the bears that possibly owned this knowe decided to come back looking for porridge. Mainly because the odds were stacked that I would be the bowl that was just right.

"Partially." Rook replied. "I followed an older transient in here because she said that she might have information about possible abductions in the area."

"And you followed her through a random hole in a fence?" I asked skeptically. "That didn't scream trap? I mean, seriously Rook! You have knowledge of a plethora of supernatural and magical creatures that lay traps like that, and that didn't occur to you?"

"Oh it did, smart ass." Rook chided. "But I wanted information and I came ready. I have read enough of your books, and I still had my iron-tipped jackets loaded, so I figured that I had a good chance of doing enough damage to escape if need be. Thankfully, I was right. The old lady was actually a hag."

I heard a shrill whistle come from Dawn as she approached the conversation. I had to agree with her assessment. Hags are nasty fae. They're inhumanly strong, almost bullet proof, with the exception of iron, and they have a multitude of magical abilities that make them pretty hard to kill. I had only killed two since getting involved in this life. I would bet money that she only lost because she didn't take him seriously as a threat. Rook's inability to react to passing through that breach in the Veil probably saved his life. Well that, and iron tipped bullets casted by me.

"The high pitched assessment of our esteemed elf is pretty accurate." I said. "She was banking on you reacting to coming through that tear in the Veil like we did. She would have probably toyed with you at her leisure while you were disoriented."

"Hags do love to play with their food." Dawn added with a nod of agreement.

"Yes, well… about that." Rook interrupted. "This particular hag got real chatty with me once I shot her in the stomach with iron. Or at least she did after I promised to ease her suffering if she answered some questions."

"What did she say?" I asked. I had not been expecting this development.

"Well, let's just say that the FBI were right to toss this one to me." Rook answered with a sigh. "Said that she loved them, if you can believe that. It was pure hero worship. They had apparently saved her and others like her from the Order."

"Oh, wonderful." I groaned. "That's just what we need, a bunch of carnivorous fae that worship and are indebted to a bunch of human psychopaths."

"Oh it's worse." Rook added.

"It always is." I replied.

"Apparently Bethlehem has her, and I am guessing the other fae like her, abduct people for them. She gave me the impression that the folks running Bethlehem feast on the people that get captured."

"Brings a whole new concept to 'hungry for faith.'" I snickered. Rook gave me a concerned look, but Dawn and I shared a tight-lip smile. "I'm sorry, that was in sinful taste."

That was apparently Dawn's breaking point, because she burst out into laughter that quickly infect both Rook and I. The three of us began laughing wildly, allowing ourselves to revel in this momentary reprieve in this horrible scenario.

"Oh there is something very wrong with us." Rook mused as he wiped a tear from the duct of his eye. "This shouldn't be this funny."

"That's what makes it funny." I replied, attempting to stifle my laughter. "It's really not funny, but we have to laugh to get through it."

"Laughter is the best medicine for almost everything." Dawn gasped between giggles. "That and sarcasm."

A silence slowly crept over the three of us as reality came crashing back in place. I nodded absently as I looked from Rook to Dawn. We all shared a telling moment, as we allowed ourselves to gain composure and shift our minds back to the task at hand.

"So you're sure that you killed her?" I asked, suddenly fearing that Rook might not have been able to finish the deed. Hags were notorious for not going down easy.

"Pretty sure." Rook answered confidently. "I put one right between her eyes, so what's left of her brain has probably drained out by now. Wait, you don't think that there could be another one that lives here too?"

"No," I answered. "Hags don't typically play well with others. Another Hag would mean that they would have to share their kill. And unless they have an offspring, they don't do that.

"That's comforting." Rook shuddered. "I thought that hags were all females, how in the hell do they reproduce then? You know what, never mind, I don't want to know. Anything that eats people is in a category of things I don't need to know."

"But it's odd…" Dawn added. "Hags prefer to eat children. So unless they are looking for someone to bear them one of their own, they don't hunt adults. And if that's the case, they capture and rape some poor sod until they conceive and then feed him to the child he helped create."

Rook began retching himself, as if the effects of passing through the Veil were finally wreaking havoc on his equilibrium and stomach. I knew of the point that Dawn made, but I was trying to save my friend the horror of this knowledge. Dawn apparently had no such dilemmas or quandaries.

"I could have gone the rest of my life without knowing that." Rook rasped between heaves. "Don't you dare tell Vergil or the Angel!"

"Not a word." I promised as I slowly guided him to the pass through the Veil.

Now we were faced with another serious problem. We had to close this tear in the Veil. Not to mention every other tear that was possibly out there because of the beasties that Bethlehem had in their service. It never rained, it poured…

"Onwards and upwards!" I chanted cheerily as I pushed Rook through the Veil. I let Dawn go before me, and then took one final look around. "Just another day in paradise."

CHAPTER 15
REFLECTIVE PROJECTIONS

I had managed to snag the location of Bethlehem's main offices from Rook's file before he left us to return to his hotel. He had mentioned something about needing a shower and a stiff drink before doing anything else, and I couldn't blame him. After all, he just found out that he was prime daddy material for a hag.

"What are you going to do from here?" Rook asked after rolling down his SUV window.

"I don't know." I lied. "I might hit the pavement and start trying to flush more of these hags and fae out of their hidey-holes."

"Don't be too stupid!" Rook barked. He looked to Dawn and softened his expression. "Please make sure you keep this idiot in line. Please!"

"Yes, sir!" Dawn replied, saluting Rook comically.

"The blind leading the blind…" Rook groaned as he started his vehicle.

Dawn and I both broke into a low giggle as Rook leaned forward and softly pounded his head against his steering wheel. He looked up and whispered something under his breath and returned his attention to the two of us as we broke into heavier laughter.

"Now, I'm serious…" Rook exclaimed. "Don't go getting yourselves killed. I don't think that I'll be able to pull this one off without you."

"Don't you worry about us." I gasped between laughs. "I was doing this for two years before I met you."

"You were leaving a trail of destruction, chaos, and massive property damage before you met me." Rook sighed. "Just… please don't blow any buildings up. Redding is known for its wildfires. I would hate to see something like that happen because you decided to pull what you did when we found her. No offense to you Dawn."

"None taken." Dawn giggled again. "So don't burn anything down and don't blow anything up."

"Right!" Rook affirmed.

He put his SUV into motion and pulled out of the parking lot, leaving the pair of us in silence under the dull yellow halo of the lights on the posts above fighting against the early evening sunlight. I followed his taillights as he departed, making sure that he was well gone before doing anything.

"So what are you really planning to do." Dawn asked breaking the silence.

"I plan on cutting the head off this snake early." I answered. "Too often Rook and I find ourselves scrambling against our enemies at the last minute; relying on Hail Marry acts of desperation and hoping for the best."

"Ok… that's still a bit vague." Dawn replied. "Let me ask again. What are WE actually going to do?"

"We're going to the offices of Bethlehem and killing the ass holes in charge!" I replied smugly. "Rook's hands are always tied by his job. But me… I am a criminal wanted for murder. Might as well give the FBI their money's worth."

"Are you sure?" Dawn asked, her voice more skeptical than worried. "These are normal humans after all."

"I'm sure." I answered. "And besides, there isn't anything normal about what these douche-bags are doing! I have no qualms about ending them. I mean, they're eating people! And not even evil people, but random people off of the streets. I mean, where is that ok?"

"When you put it that way…" Dawn laughed wickedly. "Shiny, let's be bad guys!"

"I am so hot for you right now." I said dramatically.

"Nerd!" Dawn teased loudly.

She ran off to my car and jumped onto the open window of the passenger-side door like she was an extra on the Dukes of Hazard. She crossed her arms on the roof of the Gremlin and rested her chin on her hands as she looked back at me.

"Are you coming, or what?!" Dawn asked playfully.

All I could do was grin as I jogged over to my car and leaned over the roof to meet her gaze, tempting fate to lock eyes with her again. I saw the manic truth of our world dance in her eyes and play across her grin. And all I could do in response was share in the mania and return the smile.

"So, instead of taking you out on a proper date, do you want come do the next best thing with me?" I asked mischievously.

"And what's that?" Dawn answered impishly.

"Go kill a bunch of people!" I casually and loudly replied.

As I said this, a random customer walked out of the gas station and passed close enough to the car to notice us. He looked at me warily as he moved carefully past us. Clearly he had heard me blurt out that last statement, which only added to Dawn's fit of laughter as he eyed the pair of us with extreme caution.

"Oh, not you!" I laughed as I gestured at him, shooing him along. As he got further away, I called, "Don't worry, it probably won't be anyone you know either!"

Dawn slid into the passenger seat laughing hysterically as the man got into his car and quickly left the parking lot in a hurry. I opened my door and followed her inside, enjoying the humor of the moment. I pulled my phone out, opened Google Maps, and quickly tapped the address that I had lifted from Rook's file into the search bar. I tapped the search button and let the directions pop up before starting the car.

"Are you ready to stop some bad guys?" I asked excitedly.

"I thought you would never ask." Dawn replied. "Now get this heap moving, we're losing daylight."

"As you wish!" I answered, and from there we were on our way.

It didn't take long to find the building, however without the direction from my phone's GPS and Google Maps, we would never have been able to locate this place otherwise. It was down some side street in a heavily trafficked part of Redding, however, from the look of the area, it was right on the cusp of residential neighborhoods, which worried me. Were these monsters hunting their own neighbors?

I wouldn't wait past tonight to find out. I pulled into a sparsely occupied parking area of a two story, commercial office building. The place looked like it hadn't seen any occupants in years. In fact, I was almost certain of it, as there were no signs listed on the marquee style display at the entrance of the parking lot. A metal plaque with a list of office numbers was positioned at the entrance to the building itself, with only one occupant. Bethlehem L.L.C. The letters that spelled out the company name were newer than the sign, which told me that we were in the right place.

I motioned for Dawn to grab the door and open it as I pulled my gun and casually held it at my hip. She nodded and pulled the door, allowing me to enter before her. I looked around the fluorescent lit hall with stairs off to the side. The sign at the door had said their offices took up the entire second story of the building, which made things easier for us. I had noticed that the second story offices' windows were all covered, so none could see in. I also had noted an entire lack of security cameras in the area, and had yet to notice any in the building. We were ghosts for this dire deed.

I heard the door close behind us, letting out a noise similar to the sensation and sound your ears make when they pop. Every one of my warning instincts began screaming in unison as the lights began to flicker. I began flashing back to the Order's building where I had found Dawn, and I knew that magic was afoot.

Dawn too had noticed, as her eyes began darting around and her body tensed defensively. However, she was not frozen as she had been when we were surrounded by Janet and her Prayer Circle-jerk buddies. No, Dawn was poised and ready to lash out with whatever capability that an elf possessed. And as the lights flickered a final time, I heard her inhale sharply in anticipation.

Blackness blanketed our senses for a moment, and then the room was lit again. I almost didn't recognize our immediate surroundings. I began scanning the walls and light fixtures, looking for a sign that we were still in the same building. After a moment, I knew that even though we were in the same building, things had drastically changed about our environment.

Simple sheets of glass separating us from the contents of the lower offices now stood where walls had once been placed to divide the individual offices from the hallway. On either side of us were rows of mannequins that seemed to be made of hundreds of mirrored plates of glass. The stairs seemed to have vanished, leaving only a metal frame built into the glass wall, acting as an entrance to areas with the mannequins on the other side.

I turned to leave, knowing full well that this was a bit more than I was prepared for. Behind us was another wall of glass that stood between us and the exit. There was an opening on either side, adjacent to the main entrance, leading into the areas with the mirrored mannequins. I could see what whoever had set this trap was trying to do, and I would be damned if I would just lie down and let them have their way without me fighting back.

"Get behind me." I ordered as I broke my sawed-off open and replaced the specialized rounds that had been loaded with good old fashioned buck-shot.

Dawn nodded and stepped back as I pointed my gun at the glass and steadied my aim. I pulled both triggers and released the full fury of my weapon into what I believed to be a single pain of glass that stood between us and our freedom. Oh, how I was wrong. The pellets from my shells stopped into the glass that was clearly ballistic grade. This stuff was designed to stop bullets more powerful than shotgun shells. Tiny, circular spots of cracks dotted the surface of the sheet before me. I cursed loudly as I realized that we were going to have to go through one of the rooms with those weird, humanoid constructs.

"Balls!" I swore. "I hope that you're ready for freaky and weird."

"I am an elf wandering around with a street magician wielding a shot gun." Dawn answered. "Weird is my life."

"Fair point." I replied. "Looks like we have to get past those."

I pointed at the closest mannequin with my gun. Dawn nodded her consent, and I swallowed my growing dread and tried to put on a brave face. I broke my gun open and dumped the empty casings into my hand. I pocketed them and quickly replaced them with more standard shells. I didn't want to waste any ammunition specifically made for something else if I didn't have to. I also knew that I only had one dragon's breath round on me, and I wanted to save that for last in case I needed it.

I readied my gun again and carefully entered the room on the left. I hoped against the odds that my tactic for thinking the taking the left was always right that I used in video games would pay off here. I knew that I was naïve for even considering that. The moment that both Dawn and I had entered through that doorway, the sounds of whirring and ticking could be heard all over the room. I felt my stomach clench as the noise slowly increased to multiple noises. Very quickly, the chorus of similar sounds chirped in unison as the stale air came to life beneath the pale, fluorescent lighting.

The entrance behind us was replaced with a thick, metal door, barring our exit of this room. The only way out was pressing forward and risking the encounter of what lied ahead.

I tried to move along the pane of glass behind us and lead Dawn and me straight to the exit, but was duly thwarted by another pane of glass. In the horrid lighting it was practically invisible until you were directly in front of it. I smacked it with my gun as hard as I could and followed the visual vibration all the way down to the opposite end of the room. I noticed that there was another wall that turned away from this one and ran parallel to the actual wall. This trap was getting more and more clever and dangerous with every second. Clearly Bethlehem didn't like people showing up unannounced or without an appointment.

"Double balls." I shouted, as I noticed that most direct route to the opening in the glass at the back of this room was to travel through the dead center of it.

"We have to go through the middle, don't we?" Dawn asked irritably.

"Yup." I answered. "Let's try to run through this. Maybe we can bypass all these things before they wake up."

Dawn clenched my hand in response and we both took off from the corner of where we were. It was a short sprint. With inhuman swiftness, the mannequins moved in front of us and blocked our progress forward. They stood in a V-shape formation, with one at the point moving closer than the rest. A single, mirrored oval was fixed where this things face should be, empty, barren, and waiting to reflect whomever looked within.

It bore down on us and I raised my gun to meet its advance. A cold, rigid hand shot out and grabbed my wrist painfully, and drug me to my knees by my arm. I screamed in pain and looked into the face of the construct assailing me. But what I saw was not my reflection, but the face of Janet, the leader of the group who had surrounded us at the thrift store. A well of pure fear built up in my throat and stifled my scream as mind caught up with the current events and everything fell into place.

"Do you have time to speak of our lord and savior, Jesus Christ?" the mannequin asked as it pulled me closer to its mirrored surface.

I wasn't positive, but I was pretty damn sure that I didn't want any part of me touch any of those mirrors. Terror riddled my thoughts as I struggled to break free of this magical constructs grasp. I was worried that I had doomed Dawn and myself to certain death. I was worried that Rook wouldn't be able to take these freaks down. I was worried that I would never again get to share an ale with Bromerys. Many other things rushed into my head. That was until I heard Dawn shout a word in a language that I had never heard before. Then my attention and focus was wrenched from my scrambling and was absolutely fixated on her.

"RIASUE!" Dawn cried as she pointed her index finger at the hand that held me down.

A burst of concentrated air shot from the tip of her finger like a bullet and shatter the glass arm that held onto me. A scream of unearthly proportions chimed throughout the room as I rolled backwards towards dawn and lifted my shotgun in unison. Without hesitation I unloaded both shells into the growing throng of constructs advancing towards us. The ammunition did its job well as it tore through the reflective plates that adorned each body of these mirrored golems. Shards of broken glass sprinkled the air like silver snowflakes as the first line of the damn mannequins fell.

Dawn continued shouting her word of magic, firing blasts of concentrated air at the golems as the inched towards us. I knew that she wouldn't be able to hold out long, as magic took energy to use. I also knew that this would be a good time for the dragon's breath round that I had. With practiced grace, I emptied the shells within my gun and loaded the means of our mutual escape. Dawn stood above me firing magic like a trained marksman, every spell striking solidly. But the more that she fired, the less damage her attacks did.

"Get behind me!" I shouted as I stood up and snapped my weapon closed.

Dawn stopped firing and exchanged positions with me. I stepped forward, aiming my gun to chest level, and squeezing the trigger back. The hammer fell, igniting the gunpowder and releasing the magnesium and exothermic, pyrophoric misch metal pellets in a roaring, one-hundred foot line of incendiary flames. The intense line of destruction tore through the remaining golems, leaving a wake of smoldering destruction and chaos on either side of the swath of the shot.

Dawn ran before I had a chance to react, getting ahead of me again and running straight at the opening at the back of the room. Black smoke stained the glass, showing the exact place where we needed to pass through to escape this building that housed the products of an unholy union of Neil Gaiman and Tim Burton's imagination. We made it to the opening as the remnants of the mannequin golems began to stir from their ruined heap. As Dawn and I moved along the length of the glass, we watched in horror as these monstrosities of mechanics and magic began to piece themselves back together as best they could. The end results were far more terrifying than their predecessors as jagged appendages and sharp points of glass jutted out from these grotesquely humanoid shaped metal corpses.

We hit the door running, not waiting to see if they would pursue us any further. We emerged into a warm summer evening, lit by the luminescent glow of the light pollution of the city. The faint noises of traffic greeted my ears, as I welcomed the familiar noise. We ran all the way to the Gremlin before we stopped. Both Dawn and I took a moment to catch our breath before we did anything else, but our moment of triumph was greeted with the voice of a new threat.

"Well, well, well…" a smooth a oily voice cooed as it approached us from the building behind us. "Who might you two be, and why did our defenses trigger when you entered the building?"

CHAPTER 16
FEAR AND REMEMBERANCE

Dawn was out of breath and beyond irritated. A million thoughts stampeded through her mind as she attempted to make sense of what had just happened. Danny stood near her, his presence making her feel safer than she would ever admit to him out loud. He was smug enough without that chip on his shoulder. But those thoughts were better left for another time.

She was mainly worried about the insane mirror statues that had just tried to murder them. The one that had grabbed Danny had sounded exactly like that bible-thumping bitch, Janet who led the freaks who had stopped them at the thrift store. If the two were one and the same, that meant these things were wandering the streets daily, probably preying on unsuspecting people just like the hag had been. If that was the case, Bethlehem had gone from bad to worse. It meant that they were building magical constructs on top of getting predatory fae to hunt for their sick wants.

"Well, well, well…" a snake-like voice sang from behind Dawn and Danny. "Who might you two be, and why did our defenses trigger when you entered the building?"

A shiver ran down Dawn's spine as this newcomer's voice showered over her like a thick, oily waterfall. Both Danny and her turned together to confront this threat as it sulked toward them devilishly. If cliché villain were a trope, this man had nailed the look impeccably.

Standing before them, yet keeping a clear and safe distance, was a man of average height, wearing an expensive, well tailored suit. He was a Caucasian human, with sandy-blonde hair and a well defined jaw line. He carried himself with an authority of someone who could easily sell the most jaded and cynical person beach-front property in a desert. He stood completely at ease, assured that neither Dawn nor Danny were a threat to his wellbeing.

Danny had raised his shotgun, but Dawn knew that it was empty. He did have more ammunition for it somewhere within the confines of that ridiculous velvet coat that he wore, but that didn't help the current situation. Although, Dawn didn't disagree with Danny's response, she knew it was a pointless gesture. She only hoped that the man in front of them wasn't privy to that knowledge. She was too tired and too worked up to be able to draw magic from the remedial nature surrounding them.

So their very lives possibly relied on the success of this last effort bluff. She only hoped that Danny was charismatic enough to pull it off.

"I think that you want to be speaking you piece pretty fast before I pull the other trigger and reduce that very fine suit to a pair of very fine suit-legs." Danny called out with dashing authority.

"Goodness me!" The man mocked. "I wouldn't want that. This suit is after all, very fine. And I do hate waste. You may call me Elder Zachariah. And I am merely inquisitive. I can see why the wards would have reacted to you young man. You are clearly a threat and more than you appear to be, but why did our defensive wards include your delicious companion in their response? If you were the only threat, you should have been the only one who dealt with our golems. It is a curious thing."

"Gross!" Dawn wretched in response.

"Indeed," Zachariah replied. "What are you, tender morsel? Clearly you are not human?"

"That's none of your damn business!" Danny snapped. "Now get to the part where you back off and let us be on our merry!"

"Of course." Zachariah bowed. "Please, do not let my presence deter you from your getaway. After all, you are the ones who came here with ill intent."

Dawn stepped to Danny and placed her hand on his shoulder. She knew when to get while the getting was good, and now was that time. His body was rigid and taunt with fear and adrenaline, making Dawn wonder if he even felt her hand there. She gave his shoulder a gentle squeeze hoping to get his attention. He flinched, but just barely, as his body relaxed just enough that she knew he was paying attention.

"Let's go." She whispered.

Danny only replied with a curt nod of his head as he backpedalled cautiously to the Gremlin. Dawn got in first, shutting her door behind her before reaching across to open the driver's side door. Danny climbed in quickly, slamming his door and turning over the engine immediately. He threw the gar into reverse and tore out of the parking lot like a bat out of hell. And Dawn was all the thankful for it. The further that they got away from that place, the better.

"The next time that we go back there, I'm bringing a can of gas and a box of matches!" Danny growled.

His hands were white-knuckling the steering wheel as his body was visibly trembling. Dawn didn't know if it was from rage or fear, but she didn't fault him for either. But the idea of returning to that place at all was terrifying in itself and she couldn't bring herself to even fathom it.

"Why do we need to return to that place at all?" Dawn asked, as her voice cracked from her own terror. "Why can't we just let Rook and the FBI handle it from here while we deal with the fae on the streets?"

"You didn't notice, did you?" Danny asked as his voice relaxed slightly.

"Notice what?!" Dawn answered, fearing what possible horror she had left undiscovered.

"Zachariah…" Danny answered, his voice stoic and emotionless. "He is turning into a wendigo. And if I was a betting man, I would guess that all of the elders are at this point."

Dawn felt what little color that she had drain from her as her whole body grew cold from the knowledge that she had just been told. She remembered the cries of the beast that had wandered the halls of her prison. They haunted her waking thoughts, wickedly clinging the fringes of her memories and reminding her of the nightmares that she had lived through in that destitute and horrible place.

"No… no more…" Dawn whispered.

"You don't have to come with me." Danny answered, his voice soft and caring. "But I cannot let them turn and release themselves into the city. I don't know how many there might be, but one would be devastating, let alone several. I cannot let that happen. I would understand if you cannot come, and I don't think any less of you."

His words struck her in a way that she hadn't anticipated. She felt guilty. Dawn knew that hadn't been his intention and that he was trying to be compassionate and sincere, but he was right. If those monsters finished transforming into wendigos and got out into the main population, so many innocent people would die. Dawn may not be human, but she didn't think children and other innocent humans deserved to die.

"No, we will come back." Dawn affirmed. "We will burn this place to the ground like we burned the Order's prison!"

"Okay…" Danny answered. A moment of tense silence fell in the cab of the vehicle until Danny swore loudly.

"What's wrong?!" Dawn asked, worried that there was something more that he hadn't told her.

"I just realized that we're going to have to explain this to Rook somehow." Danny replied sourly. "I really don't want to hear that man lecture me."

"Yeah he really mother hens the crap out of you." Dawn teased. "What's that about?!"

"I don't know." Danny laughed awkwardly. "But I am a grown ass man, I can take care of myself… most of the time."

"Most of the time?" Dawn questioned.

"Yeah," Danny answered, "I'll admit there are times that I can't handle everything that gets thrown at me. Like tonight. I would have been dead if it weren't for you. Thank you."

"Did you just thank a fae?" Dawn taunted. "I hear that is dangerous."

"Yeah, yeah…" Danny laughed. "All I know is you pulled through and saved my bacon back there. That was amazing. You are amazing."

"And you're a nerd." Dawn replied with a grin. "And bacon sounds fabulous. Using nature magic in an area with minimal nature takes a lot out of a girl. Let's get something to eat, I'm starved."

"There's a Denny's not too far from here." Danny suggested idly.

"Whoa, I don't know if things have changed since I was imprisoned," Dawn exclaimed, "but back in my day, people didn't go to Denny's willingly, they wound up there in shame!"

"Yeah… fair point." Danny trailed. "There's a privately owned diner near that same Denny's and they have food that is divine."

"Well, get to it!" Dawn ordered with a laugh. "But just so you know, this isn't a date."

"Gotcha." Danny laughed.

Dawn smiled and tried to let Danny's good nature push away the thoughts of tonight and the memories of her past. He wasn't an elf, but he was a good man. She deserved a moment of peace, and he made her feel comfortable in a now unfamiliar world. She leaned her head back on the headrest of the seat and closed her eyes.

"Wake me up when we get there." She instructed.

"As you wish." Danny answered.

"And stop quoting the Princess Bride." Dawn added.

"As you wish." Danny replied.

'Oh shut up!" Dawn said as she turned
her face away from him.

She didn't want him to see her smile. Like
she had said before. Danny was smug enough
without the knowledge that he was charming...
at least charming to her. Dawn smiled harder
and let her mind drift to more pleasant thoughts.

CHAPTER 17
DINE & DASH N' GRAB

We walked into the entryway to the diner together, escaping the last moments of privacy for their private smiles and jests. Immediately we were greeted by an assortment of carved bear statues made of wood. Some held signs with quips and puns related to bears while others just stared blankly through hand-carved beady eyes. I cocked an eyebrow and looked at Dawn. I wasn't sure how she was going to react to such an odd gimmick. She looked unimpressed and highly amused.

"Bears?" Dawn chuckled. "You had on chance to wine and dine me and you choose a place with bear carvings everywhere."

"Crap…" I stammered. "We can go somewhere else."

"No!" Dawn laughed. "Here is fine. I was just having a go at you."

"Are you sure?" I asked.

"Yes, you idiot." Dawn exclaimed, her voice tinged with laughter. "Now stop standing there like a moron or people are going to think that I just broke up with you or something!"

I laughed and opened the final door that led to the main part of the diner. We were greeted by a tired-looking host who took us to a part of the diner that was unoccupied. We sat down in our booth and both ordered water. As soon as she had left to get our drinks, we both started laughing again.

"See, I told you!" Dawn chortled. "She sat us over her so we don't disturb anyone if we start fighting."

"Probably," I agreed, "But the joke's on her. We both prefer to be over here away from everyone else."

"That's not the point you idiot." Dawn exclaimed. "You're not my boyfriend, and I am not some starry-eyed waif overly charmed by your wit and charisma. This is not a date. We are getting food after nearly dying."

"Right." I answered absently. "But you did want to be seated away from everyone else right?"

"Yes…" Dawn huffed. Her eyes rolled as she redirected them toward the ceiling away from me. "So, how are we going to approach dispatching Zachariah? He is on to us now and will be expecting us."

"Well," I paused as I took a deep breath, "I wasn't lying when I said a can of gas and a box of matches. We will just have to get creative about it. It's a good thing I have a few fae that owe me some favors."

"That must piss them off." Dawn snorted. "Fairy Folk owing a mortal a favor and not the other way around. It's rich! On a different note, how were you able to tell that Zachariah is turning into a wendigo? I have magical powers tied to nature and I didn't get that from him at all."

"I don't know how to explain it really." I answered. "I could just see it. Not in his physical appearance, but rather his… energy I guess. Every time light from passing cars flashed over his face, it was as if I could see the curse, just beneath his skin… waiting."

"That's unnerving." Dawn replied. She pulled her arms around herself, clearly creeped out by the very thought of Zachariah.

We were saved by the arrival of the waiter. We weren't prepared to order, but their presence was a good excuse to change the subject. I turned to look at the body standing above us, but was frozen in place by whom I saw. My stomach clenched and my voice vanished.

"Hi, my name is Lue, and I will be assisting you this evening."

"Lue…" Dawn puzzled, "What an odd name.

"Oh, it's short for Lucifer." Lucifer answered playfully. "My father had a sick sense of humor."

"Lucifer? As in Satan?" Dawn laughed.

"The Devil in the flesh, as they would say." Lucifer replied. "Now, let me tell what I am offering tonight."

"What's the catch?!" I asked. My voice was weak and cracking.

"No catch Danny my boy." Lucifer sang flamboyantly. "This one is on the house. I can't have you dying to such meek and meager foes when there are much bigger fish to fry for me."

"Wait, you're the actual Devil?!" Dawn yelped.

"Yes, precious." Lucifer answered. "Due try to keep up. You're in the big leagues now and you can't keep being shocked by little nuances such as names."

"Lay off her." I growled, finding an ember of inner fire to stoke my courage. "Now tell me what you want."

"Oh look at the big lad, thinking he is going to save her." Lucifer mocked.

The color vanished from his eyes and the lights drastically dimmed in the room as he stood to his full height. A blanket feeling of pressure fell over me uncomfortably, as I felt as if I was being suffocated by an energy that I hadn't felt since I had been lost in the Veil itself.

"I am Lucifer, the Morningstar!" Lucifer commanded. "I am not some haughty fae that you can bully, nor am I my little brother who treats you as if you aren't beneath him. Because rest assured, Danyael MacClaude, you are. I control forces that you cannot fathom and have spoken with entities that would cause your mind to explode in their very presence. Do not fuck with me!"

I wasn't sure that I would be able to speak, even if I had wanted to. When the big bad of a pantheon that still has prayer and worship throws his weight around, to step out of the ring entirely. I had grown accustomed to speaking to Azrael and I forgot that these were freaking angels that I had been dealing with. I was way out of my weight class by challenging them. And that's what my sleight had essentially done.

"Now, if we are done with this dick measuring contest," Lucifer said, releasing his energy and allowing me to breathe normally, "because rest assured, I would win, I can tell you why I am even bothering to come to this pitiful little city."

"Yeah, sorry… my bad." I said frailly.

"Indeed it is entirely, 'your bad!' Now back to the matter at hand." Lucifer said snidely. "I have come to warn you that you're being followed. I cannot tell you who, or specifically where the person following you is, because of Daddy's direct involvement rule, but I can say that they have some nefarious plans with your delicious elven lover, Dawn."

"I'm not his lover." Dawn managed to rasp out.

"Oh please, darling." Lucifer smiled widely. "You reek of hormones and his scent is still permeating from your last tumble. Be honest with me. After all, I am the Devil. If you can't be truly honest with me, then who can you? Besides, Danny boy here isn't that bad. He has the will to resist a succubus and has done so successfully. He's a catch."

Before I knew what was happening, Lucifer had leaned down, grabbed my chin, and kissed my full on the mouth. I was unable to fight back nor struggle, as I was paralyzed with fear in the moment. His tongue slipped in and that was where I regained control and pulled away.

"My, my!" Lucifer laughed as if out of breath. "That was something too! Trust me sweetness. He may not be an elf, but he is something worthwhile. Now, my work here is done. Off I go."

And as fast as he had appeared, he was gone and our new waiter came walking in. He looked between Dawn and I and said that he would come back in a few minutes. We nodded in agreement and thanked him silently.

"What the hell was that?!" Dawn snapped. "You get warnings from the Devil?!"

"No not usually…" I grumbled. "In fact that is only the second time that I have dealt with him in person."

"But he was so chummy with you?" Dawn observed. "Hell, he kissed you! Did he slip you tongue, because it looked like he did?"

"Don't," I held up a hand, "Please… just don't. Let's not mention that again."

"Okay" Dawn agreed, clearly stifling a laugh, "but what about his warning?"

"I figured someone might." I answered. "If one of their elders came out to see us, it was to be expected. But they won't try anything in here, and we need to eat. So, let's order some food and cross that bridge when the time comes."

Dawn nodded and we moved on with the night from there. Our waiter returned and we both ordered a steak dinner with all of the trimmings, clearly both as famished as the other. We ate in relative silence, focusing on our meals rather than the fact that the Devil had just swung by to give us a warning that left the looming prospect of danger lingering over our meal. After about thirty minutes of absolute silence, I realized that our waiter hadn't come to check on us and that the whole diner was completely still. The only noise that I hear was the air conditioning pouring out from the ducts above. There were no sounds of the grill, no hushed chatter of other patrons. Only silent stillness.

"Get up carefully," I said quietly, "and stay away from the windows."

"You noticed it too?" Dawn asked as she palmed her steak knife in one hand and her fork in the other.

"Yeah." I replied. "This diner is getting ready to get slammed."

As if on cue, a body jumped through the large, picture-frame window in the dining area that we were sat in. As it landed, I caught a glimpse of blue flesh beneath its tactical clothing, and my stomach lurched in a panic as my mind immediately jumped to the thought of an ice giant. But then, I realized that the assailant was too small. This made stomach seize further as a memory came flooding back to me from a highway in Sacramento.

"Crap, crap, crap!" I shouted as I grabbed Dawn by the wrist and tried to get her to the hall so we could bottleneck this fight. I knew that we would have been dead before we got through the door if I had tired for an escape.

"What do you mean, crap?!" Dawn shouted. "There's only one person."

"That's not a person!" I yelled. "That's a fae, and they belong to the Phoenix Clan!"

"The Phoenix what?!" Dawn snapped.

"The Phoenix Clan!" I repeated as I pushed her into the hallway that was an immediate turn out of the area we had just been. "They are a clan of fae assassins. And they really don't like me."

"Is there anyone amongst the Divided Courts of the Fae that does?!" Dawn shrieked in irritation.

"Not many." I answered as I slipped my hands into my pockets and fished around for my iron-knuckles.

I knew that I wouldn't have time to load my gun and that these were my best bet to do enough damage to give me a fighting chance. My fingertips found my weapons, and I slid the familiar weights over each of my fingers. I coiled my fist around the grip and brought them out just in time to throw a punch at the Phoenix Assassin as his head came around the corner.

Now let me paint a picture for you. Real fighting is nothing like you see in movies. It's sloppy and frantic and typically you will throw at least ten punches and maybe two will actually hit. But then there's the catch of them hitting where you wanted or actually how you intended. This first strike did none of that. It went wildly past his head, giving the assassin to strike at my underarm. He thrust his short dagger at my armpit, clearly wanting to take me out of the picture immediately. And if it weren't for the enchantments on my coat, he would have. His blade didn't pierce through the cloth, but it did strike true.

My arm collapsed immediately. It felt like I had just been punched with a steel police baton, except that police baton was hitting as hard as Mike Tyson's strongest punches. I screamed in pain, but kept pushing my attack. With what little control that I had left of the arm, I feebly swung it chaotically at the assassin. He clearly was bewildered by this, because he paused for the briefest of moments, confused by my tactic, which created an opening for me to strike. Or rather, Dawn to. As I prepared to throw my left hand out in a strong hook, Dawn lunged around me, lashing out with her dinner fork and stabbing the Phoenix Assassin in their left eye.

I heard the sound of bond crunching as Dawn clearly nicked the cheek bone but kept driving the makeshift weapon through. A bloodcurdling scream erupted from our assassin for the evening, as they staggered back in clear agony. I mean, come on… you would be in agony too if someone stabbed you in the eye with a fork.

I fell back and took the opportunity to load my gun. I let my injured arm find the handle and pull out my weapon as my other grabbed two iron shot shells from my belt. I placed the cases in my mouth and flicked the gun open. I tucked the weapon under my injured arm and shove the shells in place and then grabbed it and flicked it closed.

I walked to the assassin and took the head shot. His body fell to the floor leaving a mess of blood and spatter all over the bear statues with their empty stares nearby. I motioned for Dawn to follow as we walked past the body an out the front door. I knew the sound of my gun would be drawing some unwanted attention and I didn't want to be anywhere near here when the cops arrived. As we exited the building and stepped into the parking area, we were threatened with the falling of footsteps behind us.

"Oh balls!" I said exasperatedly.

Janet and her prayer circle lackeys were approaching from around the building. I could hear Dawn almost yelp as she started to breathe heavily. The group of nine women approached at a mechanical but quick pace, resolving any doubts that remained that these were the mirrored golems that had nearly killed us.

"We would like to speak with you lady friend about the One True God." Janet announced as she power walked her way towards us menacingly.

"Oh, go to hell!" I spat as I pointed the shotgun at her face and emptied the chamber.

The sounds of metal wrenching and glass crunching filled the night as her body kept moving without the head. I swore loudly as I turned to Dawn. I tossed her my keys.

'Get to the car and go!" I shouted as I returned my attention to the golems.

I held my fists up and just started swinging. There was no rhyme no reason to my punches, just furry and terror. I threw my whole body into my attacks, but the group wasn't focused on me. I hit every single one of the damn constructs that tried to pass me, each strike ringing with the sound of broken glass. But they didn't stop. But then, a sound of hope grinded out into the night. The Gremlin was awake and in gear. Dawn had managed to put the car and gear and turn it around. My heart jumped at the sight, feeling that we might have a chance to get out of this alive.

I heard the tires squeal as Dawn stepped on the accelerator and the car took off. I dove out of the way as she made way to plow into the mirrored golems and drive to freedom. But then something happened that I couldn't expect. Every one of the golems stood together and caught the front end of my car and stopped it dead in its tracks. My heart sank into my stomach as I realized that I was now nowhere near enough to the fray to do anything. But that didn't stop me from trying. I ran at full sprint as the mirrored golem at the back of the group broke away from the pack and walked straight to the driver's window. The sounds glass exploded into the night air as the pieces of the window rained into the car and all over Dawn.

The golem reached into the car and seized a hold of the front of Dawn's shirt, pinning her against the seat. It then leaned into the car, placing its face directly in front of Dawn's. I ran faster, willing my body to push itself hard to make it to Dawn before anything else could happen. I was too late. The golem dropped its glamour that made it look human, revealing its true appearance. The same mannequin-like construct that we had seen earlier this evening was now a breath away from Dawn, the mirror where its own face should be perfectly reflecting the expression of terror painted across Dawn's visage.

It leaned forward and pressed its reflective surface against Dawn's face. And then, she was gone. The golem pulled itself from my car, as the rest of its comrades set the car down allowing it to roll into the diner building, where it was stopped. It hadn't been doing that fast by this point so there wasn't any further damage to the building or the Gremlin.

The mirrored golems turned and walked towards the sidewalk, and just vanished into the night, as if fading away into nothingness. Sometimes magic was a bitch. I was left alone and in a panic. I couldn't stand around here and wait, I had to leave. I ran to my car and made a get-away as fast as I could. The hot, summer air stung at my face as the speed from my car shot it at me as I drove. And then, something else happened that was completely unexpected. I ran out of gas.

My car drifted to the side of the road where I dropped my head against the steering wheel and swore loudly. Dawn had just been taken by a church of people turning into wendigos. People that like to eat other people. I needed help. I had to get her back. And then I did something that I wasn't sure that I would ever do. I prayed.

"Azrael…" I whispered to the emptiness of the night. "I need your help."

"I'm sure you do." Azrael answered from my back seat. "Now tell me, what has happened."

CHAPTER 18
SHATTERED GLASS

"They took Dawn!" I shouted at the angel in my back seat.

"Who took Dawn?" Azrael answered.

"Bethlehem's magical mannequins!"I yelped. "They took her and I couldn't stop them. Lucifer warned me that they were coming, and I still wasn't able to stop them."

"My brother was here?" Azrael asked, his voice piquing interest.

"Yes!" I yelled. "And he warned me. He practically laid it out for me, and I wasn't smart enough to see the facts."

"Please, start from the beginning." Azrael instructed calmly. "I need all of the information before I can say whether or not that I could help you."

So I spent the next few minutes catching the former arch angel of Death up on what had transpired in his absence. He inquired the most about Bethlehem and Lucifer's involvement. I had a growing feeling of dread that he wasn't going to be much help, but at this point. I was willing to take what I could get.

"I should have realized the Lucifer could have easily mentioned the Phoenix Clan assassin!" I snapped bitterly. "Angels don't have rules that keep them from interacting with the fae! I should have guessed that there was more at play in his warning."

"Yes, you should have." Azrael agreed. "However, Lucifer seemed to be intentionally distracting you while he gave you this warning. That is his way. In fact, the only reason he can interact with you as directly as he does is because of your debt through me."

"I get that, thanks." I growled. "I don't know what I can do. Help me, please!"

"I know that you asking for help is a very difficult thing for you to do." Azrael replied. "But because this Bethlehem is led by mortals, my involvement is limited at best."

"That's not good enough!" I shouted as I punched the steering wheel. "You ran with me all of this time while we were hunting for Eve! What's so different here?!"

"Eve is pregnant with a Nephilim." Azrael answered coolly. "My Father decreed that they cannot exist and this one is of my direct lineage. There is circumstance that enables me to act directly."

"But you can't put a stop to a bunch of psychotic, cannibalistic church zealots." I spat. "What good is your God? What good are you? Hell, this is why atheists exist."

"I can take you to fetch Stephen Hightower," Azrael sighed. "And then I can transport you to where you need to go."

"Why not Vergil?!" I sapped. "Is he too good to help now?"

"Vergil is otherwise occupied on an errant for me." Azrael replied. "My search for Eve and the unborn Nephilim continues."

"Of course…" I sighed in frustration. "Let's go get Rook. But first, you are going to take me to gather supplies. I'm going to need to make some more dragon's breath rounds."

Azrael arched his eyebrow, clearly not understanding my intent. But he nodded in consent and we were off. He dropped the Gremlin off at the castle, where I left my call stone that I used to summon the gremlins that fix it signaling for their assistance. I left a note with explanations and warned them of the shattered glass and two six-packs of Yoo-hoo. It was their preferred method of payment. Most fae had their addiction to sweets, and Yoo-hoo was the gremlins' treat of choice.

After I squared things at home, we moved on to gathering the ingredients for the dragon's breath shotgun shells. Having an angel that could zap you anywhere was helpful, especially when you were looking for hard to acquire materials for highly illegal and dangerous ammunition for an equally illegal sawed-off shotgun. It was short work with Azrael's help. And as soon as we had everything, I asked Azrael to take us somewhere safe and open.

"Why are we here?" Azrael puzzled as he took in our surroundings.

"Because, I need you to take these ingredients and combined them into what I need." I answered.

"You want me to make weapons for you?" Azrael asked carefully.

"No, I want you to make ammo for me. Sort of." I replied. "I don't have the time to put this many together safely. However, I know that you can. You're not doing anything against our contract. I will be using these frequently, even for you. All you are doing is rearranging the ingredients into the empty shell in a manner that they do what I need them to."

"You ask too much of me." Azrael answered, his voice adopting a tone of anger. "This will be the last and only time that I will do this for you. Any weapons created from my power will be touched by it. I fear the results of creating such dangerous things in such a way. Be warned that I will remove them from your possession if I deem they are too dangerous."

"Whatever, just please get to it." I said.

"You speak to me so profanely." Azrael injected as I felt his energy build slowly. "I am an arch angel, and as Lucifer said, you would do well to remember that. I endure your sleights because I know that you fight a battle that others cannot and that you have suffered more than most. But those facts will only anchor you safely in the harbor of my good graces for so long."

"Is that a threat." I asked, wondering if I had pushed the angel too far tonight.

"No, a simple fact." Azrael answered. "Angels do not deal in threats. We offer absolutes and facts."

"Only a Sith deals in absolutes." I mocked, trying to lighten the mood.

"Are you comparing angels to the evil space wizards in George Lucas' fable?" Azrael hummed. It almost sounded like amusement.

"Just observing." I joked. I felt his energy dwindle and vanish. "Are you done?"

"The deed is done." Azrael answered dryly.

The angel stepped in front of me, his arms bent at ninety degree angles and his hands held aloft. He hefted a leather, shoulder-waist bandoleer in his grasp. Every slot was fitted with a shell, each one seemingly cast in the whitest gold. I gave Azrael a quizzical look as I pulled one of the shells out to inspect it.

"Gold?" I inquired as I sized the ammunition up.

"I don't think so." Azrael answered as he took the shell from me. "It's platinum actually. Interesting. I'm not sure what happened here. But if I had to venture a guess, my power transmuted the material of the casing to the purest metal that you know of."

"Shiny!" I said idly as I slipped the casing back in its loop. I took the bandoleer from Azrael and fastened it in place quickly. "There should be more shells."

"I took the liberty of sending them to your boxes of munitions at your temporary lodgings." Azrael commented.

"Good idea." I said. "Now let's go get Rook."

Azrael stepped forward and placed his hand on my shoulder, and we were traveling again. In the moment that it took me to exhale, we were in the kitchenette of some motel with a shocked Rook standing a few feet in front of us. In one hand he was holding an open can of ravioli with a fork in it, and a glass of amber liquid in the opposite. He was wearing boxer shorts and a white undershirt, with his shoulder holster still strapped on over it.

Clearly he hadn't been expecting company, because the man expelled a very un-man-like noise from his mouth and dropped the glass. The sounds of breaking glass was muffled by Rook's audible proof of his moment of shock.

"Good freaking god, MacClaude!" Rook blustered. "What the hell?!"

"I need your help." I interrupted. "Bethlehem took Dawn."

"What?! Why? When?" Rook fumed. "Tell me what in the hell happened!"

I felt the solid lump materialize in my throat as I knew what was coming. My heart sank and I knew that I didn't want to Rook to think less of me. And for the first time, I realized that I thought of him as family. I cared about him and looked up to him. He was the type of man that I had thought that I had wanted to be growing up. And his opinion mattered to me. I heard his voice tell me to sack up in the back of my head, and I obliged. I swallowed the lump in my throat and began telling him what had happened.

His face never gave anything away as he listened intently, only stopping me to get key details about the building layout and the golems themselves. When I finished speaking, he walked to me and stood directly in front of me with a frown. And even though I knew that it was probably coming, it still surprised me when he smacked me upside my head.

"What the hell were you thinking?!" He growled. "I told you not to do anything stupid. And you did. Well, are you ready to this the hard way now?"

"Yeah, if you're willing to help." I replied. "I cannot do this alone."

"Of course you can't, you idiot!" Rook laughed sardonically. "And of course I will help. Heaven knows that you shouldn't have to go this alone."

"They do, indeed." Azrael added from the background.

"I take it the divine power is sitting this one out?" Rook grunted questioningly.

"Yeah," I answered, "He can't get involved because Bethlehem is ran by humans."

"That's what I had figured." Rook sighed. "Can he at least give us a lift?"

"You may tell Agent Hightower that I would be glad to give you both a lift." Azrael instructed me curtly.

"Well at least there's that." Rook huffed. "Vergil sitting this one out?"

"Yes, again." I sighed. "Apparently he is working for Azrael right now."

"Well, I have had to work with worse odds." Rook chuckled. "Ok, let me get dressed and we can leave. Wait, what type of shells are those?"

"The illegal kind." I replied patting the leather strapped over my shoulder.

"Say no more." Rook groaned. "And Danny…"

"Yeah?" I answered.

"Clean this damn glass up." Rook ordered. "Also, you owe me a bottle of Scotch."

Rook exited through a door off to the side of the room, leaving Azrael and I alone.

"I don't suppose that you could just zap this away, could you?" I asked the angel.

"No, I don't think that I will." Azrael replied calmly. "A little labor is good humility, and humility is good for the soul. And it builds character too."

I rolled my eyes and began looking for a way to clean up the shards of alcohol drenched glass. And I'll be damned if I didn't hear Azrael chuckle behind me… like an ass hole. I laughed along with him, as I tried not to think about what Dawn was going through right now.

CHAPTER 19
RELICS OUT OF PLACE

Given the business that I am in, one would assume that discovering that some old wives' tale about mystical mumbo jumbo wouldn't faze me at this point. Well, I can assure you that they would be wrong. Because, sometimes I am completely blown away by new discoveries of the magical variety.

Azrael had transported Rook and I to a completely different area from where I had encountered Zachariah and the mirrored golems earlier this evening. We now stood in front of some garish, eight-foot, chain-link fenced construction zone with black plastic fastened to the fencing itself. Apparently, Bethlehem didn't want anyone looking inside. A nearby sign promised new, low-income housing was being developed here, but something told me that was a lie. And anyone who dares trespass became a missing person.

Yet, trespassing was on our agenda this evening. Probably destruction of property, or as Rook's people liked to call it; felony arson. They seemed to have this misconception that I was some pyromaniac that liked to maliciously burn down people's property.

However, that isn't true. Fire just happens to be the best way to make sure you kill everything in a structure and cleanse the area in case of dealing with the undead. Or in most cases, the things I fight seem to enjoy trying to set me on fire and things get out of hand. Either way, I don't enjoy burning people's property down… but I would tonight. Whatever was being built on the other side of that fence was going to be reduced to a mass of rubble and cinders when we got Dawn back. And I would make sure that every member of Bethlehem was inside when it was burning.

I felt the energy within me stir in anticipation. The same energy that I had used to destroy the prison that Dawn had been held in. Something about it was excited. No, I was excited about the prospect of destroying this place… these people, no these beasts! I let the thought dance within, filling me with adrenaline. I stepped forward and pointed my gun at the chain securing the gate of the fence.

"Knock Knock!" I shouted as I pulled the trigger.

The lance of white and blue fire that lashed out was blinding. The intense heat of it turning the mixed metals of the fence, chain, and lock to butter made me step back, not wanting to singe my upper layer of skin. The shell quieted and extinguished, leaving the scents of melted plastic and burning soil painted in the air. As the smoke cleared, a wide hole in the fence large enough for a man to walk through became visible between the now sagging and swaying remnants on the chain-link gate.

"Bit overkill, don't you think?" Rook remarked.

"Hell no!" I retorted snidely as I ejected the now empty shell from the barrel. "These bible black ass clowns have it coming."

"Ok…" Rook drawled. "I was going to ask how you wanted to do this, but apparently we're using your standard destroy everything until they come looking for us method."

"Why fix what isn't broken?" I laughed.

"Because it is broken when you're done." Rook groaned. "As is many other things that weren't a part of the plan. Your collateral damage is ridiculously high sometimes."

"Bill me." I replied as I reloaded the shell and snapped my gun closed. "Now, I believe there is mischief afoot and I plan on partaking."

"I'm not sure if that's an actual quote from your nerd shows or not." Rook commented.

"And you'll never know." I added gleeful as I stepped through the now open gate.

Now, the signs all said that they were building low income housing behind these walls, but my eyes told me another story. All I could see was cement and cinder block walls running the inner length of the fence which skirted the entire property. There was about a six foot space between the fence and the wall, just enough room for one to two men to walk around and work. I could feel a buzzing pressure in my ears, which told me there was an enchantment at work that had to do with silence and noise. I have had my fair share of run-ins with these, and they were usually used to keep the sounds of an area from escaping to the rest of the world. Human magic users typically had them cast over their sanctuaries to keep normal folks from hearing the odd and often dangerous things that transpired where magic dwelled.

I could only guess what Zachariah and Bethlehem used them for. I heard Rook's feet crunching on gravel behind me, so I was sure that it wasn't going to silence us inside. He came and stood next to me, taking in the odd structure in front of us.

"Well, that's odd." Rook whistled as he looked down both walls. "Never a dull moment with you, MacClaude."

"Yup." I confirmed. "Just a heads up, there's an enchantment that traps the sounds that happen on this side of that gate within its confines. So, there's no need to play quiet tonight."

"That's disturbing." Rook huffed. "Why would ordinary humans running a homeless outreach program need something like that?"

"Indeed." I answered. "Let's go ask someone shall we?"

Rook nodded and we started walking to the left of the entry, hoping to find a door or some guard that could at least be aggressively persuaded into disclosing some directions to us. I was really hoping to put some major emphasis on the aggressively.

Moments passed as Rook and I both continued to shift our points of view to watch our backs. I soon became annoyed with this continuing, bad cliché of a buddy cop trope and picked up a rock to throw at the wall. That was until I noticed two gargoyle statues perched at separate intervals on the wall further down. Or rather, Rook noticed and grabbed my wrist to keep me from throwing the rock. He pointed his gun that the statues silently as he stepped past me with a judgmental sigh.

The gargoyles were simple in design, but seemingly ancient and very large. These were not garden or lawn ornaments that you could buy only. These were hand carved and transplanted to this location for a specific purpose. What that purpose was, I did not know. But even in their simplicity, the gargoyles were elegant and extravagant compared to the pillars and walls that they sat atop.

"Well what do you suppose these are here for?" Rook asked quietly as he surveyed the gargoyles.

"I don't know." I replied as I eyed the pair of stone relics carefully. "I mean, I know gargoyles were meant the protect buildings from evil entering and what not, but look at these two. Not only are they out of place on this mass produced, throw together wall, but they aren't even facing outward. Their gazes are staring at the inside of this opening."

"Maybe they are here to keep evil from escaping." Rook suggested grimly.

"Maybe," I agreed, "But if that's the case, what the hell are they trying to keep in?"

I have horrible timing for telling questions. I really do. As I finished asking this question, both gargoyles lifted their heads in unison and released the most awful sound that I have heard in a while. The only comparison that I could relate to it was grinding stone on cast iron. The wrenching noise of the gargoyles sang into the night and I was now privy as to why Bethlehem needed the noise trapping enchantment. Also, I now knew what gargoyles were keeping in.

Wendigos… a whole hell of a lot of wendigos.

"CRAP, CRAP, CRAP…" Rook stammered loudly as we both fell backwards as the mass of pale, lithe giants lunged for the exit.

I wasn't sure how, but the gargoyles just glared down at the monsters and they retreated as if they were terrified and whipped. It was the strangest thing, because from what I knew, wendigos didn't do that for anything or anyone. There wasn't a non-divine creature amongst the fae, humans, undead, nightbreed, or demons that would call a wendigo to heel like that. Yet these two four foot nothing gargoyles held near a dozen wendigos at bay like it was easy.

"Crap is right, my rotund growing friend." I said in awe. "But let's not waste this opportunity."

"What opportunity?!" Rook shouted.

I let my next few actions speak for themselves. I walked to the opening between the two gargoyles and let the wendigos see me. I knew that even with the looming presence of their big bad glaring down at them, they would be unable to resist fresh meat. Like moths to the flame the whole swarm of them got up and piled towards me, desperately reaching at me past the wicked glare of their jailors.

As soon as I felt that the group of them was lined up enough, I pointed my gun and squeezed the trigger. The spout of flame sand out like an operatic dragon roaring in triumph. The smell of rotted flesh burning soon joined the remnant stenches of the fence and plastic from earlier. The wendigos all roared in agony as the fire arched through their bodies as if they were made of tissue paper. Their masses burned into nothingness like tinder drenched in gasoline until all that remained was the faint echoes of their other-worldly voices.

I knew my work was done because the gargoyles returned to their former positions of sculpted sentinels ominously warning evil not to approach. Rook walked forward to join me, looking at the greasy burn on the wall in front of us.

"Why didn't you bring that with you when we found Dawn?" He asked somberly.

"Because I thought that we were going to be dealing with the Order of Saint Patrick and not a building full of ghosts and a wendigo."I spat. "Besides, I knew that you would lecture me about the legality of these if you knew that I had access to them."

"Legal matters are the furthest from my mind right now." Rook admitted. "I'm more worried about you burning this damn county to the ground. This whole area is well known for its wild fires."

"Don't worry pops," I laughed, "I'll be careful. I already have Azrael telling me that he will take these shells from me if he thinks they're too dangerous."

"That's a comforting thought." Rook replied flatly. "Just be careful, kid."

"Got it." I answered with a salute. I absently clicked my gun open and reloaded the shell as we peered around the corners.

"What the hell is this place?" Rook asked as he took in the structure around us.

"It's a goram labyrinth!" I hissed. "Those nut jobs actually built a labyrinth to hide their members who turn into wendigos."

"Can you get through this?" Rook asked.

"Actually…" I answered as I began rummaging through my inner pocket before emerging with a piece of chalk, "believe it or not, this happens a lot when dealing with the fae, so I started carrying chalk with me."

"How is that supposed to help exactly?" Rook inquired skeptically.

"We mark our path as we go, that way if we get turned around we know which ways we have been already." I answered.

"Sounds good, lead the way." Rook instructed.

"Why me?" I asked.

"Because you have the fancy fireworks that can kill a wendigo, and I have a pee shooter in comparison." Rook scoffed.

I laughed and marked the wall and turned into the maze in front of us. I knew that things were just getting interesting this evening. I only hoped that they didn't get any worse.

CHAPTER 20
OF MEN, MONSTERS, & MAZES

Apparently the elders of Bethlehem had little faith in their own people's abilities to navigate their labyrinth when they had it built, because Rook and I were walking through this like it was cake walk. Or perhaps there was something else afoot here. Perhaps the magic of this structure was only designed to keep the wendigo in. Whatever the reason, it made navigating it a breeze.

However there was another detail that I was noticing about the labyrinth's design. The closer to its center that Rook and I got, the deeper into the earth that we went. We had been on a downward descent for a while now and I was beginning to worry what was waiting for us when we defeated it.

"Is this just a little bit too cliché, or am I imagining things." I remarked as we hustled around another blind corner.

"Cliché?" Rook laughed. "That's rich coming from you. You're several stereo-typed clichés rolled into one!"

"That's my point." I huffed irritably. "This is too cliché, even for my standards."

"This maze was probably designed to keep whoever was dumb enough to enter it distracted until they were either eaten or were lost enough to become the second course for the elders."

"That is so wrong on so many levels." I shuddered.

I slowed down to catch my breath and my wits, allowing Rook to gain a slight lead ahead of me. I was worried about Dawn and I was worried about leaving this place standing. I wasn't sure that if we stuck around to fight them off we would survive the fight. So, my goal was to get Dawn and get out before we all died.

"Eyes up!" Rook called from ahead. "You've got to see this."

I rounded the corner and found myself staring at a structure that was built into the ground itself. Sure, there were some walls and decorative stuff above ground, but Rook and I could clearly see a stairway leading down into an unseen walkway below. The entrance was at the dead center of the structure, the handrails jutting upward from the opening below.

"Ok, who wants to be the first one to enter the creepy dungeon that belongs to cannibals?" I laughed nervously.

"Lead on, hero!" Rook mocked.

"We've been through this, I'm no hero." I snapped back.

"Fine… lead on, lover boy!" Rook replied smugly.

"Sometimes, I really hate you." I chided in defeat.

"Get over it." Rook ordered. "This won't be a Disney movie we're walking into. The bad guys will either try to kill us, or eat us. Given our track record, probably both."

"Oh, don't I know it." I replied. "We live such interesting lives."

"Shut up and get in the damn dungeon." Rook barked as he attempted to stifle his laughter, as it turned into a dry cough.

I obliged my friend to keep him from dying from asphyxiation. His smoking was going to kill him before any of the monsters that we dealt with did.

As I ducked into the opening, my eyes immediately protested this drastic change in lighting. My vision blurred as it struggled to pull in any vestiges of illumination in this shadowy passage before us. I could hear Rook curse in shrill whispers as he ran into the same problems that I now faced. I could barely make out the form of my friend in the dim atmosphere. I pulled out my cell phone and turned on the flashlight feature. I lifted it above my head, attempting to light the area so that we didn't break our necks on the walk down.

"I keep forgetting that phones can do that now." Rook huffed as he got closer to me.

"Yeah, it's handy." I commented. "Let's keep going."

I moved forward into the depth of this dark and creepy hole. The walls were made poured cement. So this was built to suit Bethlehem's needs and they hid it under their construction areas. No one would think twice about hearing construction noises at a construction site. And if they didn't, well that wasn't unheard of either. Many sites get shut down for little things like zoning and permits. It was a perfect hiding place.

Rook and I traveled in relative silence as we descended into the black. We had seen no door, no other path to take since we entered. It seemed that we had to be at least fifty feet below by this point, which was absurd. The only times you heard of things being built l that deep underground was in bad spy or cheesy conspiracy movies. It just didn't happen in the real world. Or least it hadn't. Here I was walking down stairs that led to some underground lair of an evil organization that eats people. That sounded like a bad Sci-fi movie itself.

At some point on the way down, Rook had managed to step in front of me, which didn't seem important at the time. It was now. He suddenly held up his hand in a clenched fist, which I guess was him signaling me to stop. This would have been great if I had been paying attention. I wasn't. I kept walking, oblivious to Rook's hand and ran straight into his back. It was at this moment that physics and gravity took over and we both rolled down several feet of stairs, coming to rest at an open walk in front of a heavy steel door. I groaned in pain as I untangled my limbs and coat from Rook and attempted to push away from his heavier mass. As I peeled our bulks apart, I only hoped that I hadn't injured Rook. He was my only friend and I couldn't live with myself if something happened to him and it had been my fault.

"Rook, are you ok?" I asked as I looked over at his prone form.

He didn't answer, but he did groan and roll over and flipped me off as he pushed himself to his knees.

"What the hell was that?" He croaked.

"Sorry, I wasn't paying attention." I replied.

"Get your head in the game MacClaude!" Rook barked. "Christ on a cracker, it's like working with children."

We both stood up and gave the door a once over. It was solid, built for security. Or in this case, to keep wendigos from breaking through it. This led to the discovery that it was obviously locked. A series of foul language engulfed the air as both Rook and I vented our frustrations outwardly. Finally, I made a decision and began searching along the door's middle section to locate where the locking mechanism met the doorframe. It was a quick find. I checked to see that my gun was chambered, and gave a quick count of remaining shells in my bandoleer. Once satisfied, I pointed my gun at the point of connection.

"You're going to want to stand back for this." I announced to Rook. "In fact, it would probably be best if you turned around and closed your eyes."

"What are you doing?" Rook inquire, clearly worried.

"I'm going to shoot the lock off." I answered flatly. "It's probably going to take a while. Hopefully I don't lose my gun in the process."

"Oh crap!" Rook managed to say before I fired off the first of the dragon's breath rounds.

I had the barrel pointed close enough to the door to get the job started. The arch of magnesium fueled fire lanced out and splashed over the metal of the door and its frame. I saw the metal turn black and then began to glow as the fire licked against its surface. The fire died quickly, and I ejected the shell and reloaded in quick succession. I repeated the process, heating the door where I knew it was fastened and locked in place. The fire died out, and I reloaded as I had just moments before. This process reoccurred for two more rounds before I had melted through the out layer of steel on the door and through the inner workings of the lock itself.

After the fifth shell died, I heard the groaning of super heated metal protesting against the cold air of being underground. Something inside the door snapped, heralding the sounds of my victory against the door. I stepped back to admire my handy work as the weight of the door and the vacuum of air that I had caused in the area pulled the door open slowly. I turned around to give Rook a smug look, only to find him sweating profusely and looking terrible.

"Are you ok?!" I asked.

"I'll be fine." Rook panted. "I just need to get some fresh air."

If he had intended to quell my worries, Rook failed. He attempted to stand up, only to collapse onto the floor. I raced to him, hoping that he was ok. I needed him to be ok. And for the second time that evening, I did the unthinkable. I asked an angel for help.

"Azrael!" I pleaded in earnest. "Please, I need your help. Please, I am begging you. I know that you don't technically have any reason to help me, but please. Rook needs help. He's the only family I have left."

"I know." Azrael answered. "I cannot help this time Danyael. I have extended myself in this affair too much as it stands. If Agent Hightower is to die, it will be his time. But surely, I am not the only being you know that can help with this?"

"You're right!" I answered irritably. I turned to glare at Azrael, but he was gone. Had he even been there at all? "Don't worry Rook. I have gotten so caught up in this religious bull crap; I forgot that I have other friends with powers. I just hope he answers a cold call from me."

I pulled the chalk from my pocket and began hurriedly drawing a circular pattern on the ground. I reached into the hidden breast pocket inside my coat and withdrew my old flask and set it in the center of the circle. I knew that there was still liquor in it, because I kept it filled for emergencies. Like setting fires or squashing emotional pain. Now it was going to be used to save Rook's life.

"Oh child of Mirth and Merry, son of the Nature King." I began chanting. "Come and join in on our folly, unto you I summon thee. Come drink our draught ye Nature's son, and join our revelry. And with this chant, I speak your name, Bromerys I summon thee!"

I did not know what would happen. I had no ritual fire and I was underground. I only hoped that my connection to Bromerys was strong enough to reach the old stag. I felt my stomach knot horribly as I felt the seconds tick by like hours.

"Damn it all, this place reeks of wendigo shit and death!" A voice bellowed as the sound of hooves clopping on cement greeted me.

My friend had come. Bromerys had come when I called. Tears welled in my eyes as the demi-god came into sight at the base of the stairs. He was exactly as I remembered him. His very energy teaming with good feelings and mirth. The scent of elderberry wine and fresh cut grass permeated the air as he neared me.

"Danny!" Bromerys shouted gleefully. "You look like Cerberus swallowed you and then shit you back out. You also smell like an elf bedded you several times. Good for you, they are fun."

"Bromerys, I don't have time to catch up." I bellowed. "Rook needs help fast. I don't want him to die. Can you help him?"

Bromerys walked over to Rook's prone body, giving him a visual once over and sniffing the air around him. After a moment he stooped to see my face clearly. A warm smile played over his face, driving away a bit of my own terror.

"I will help your friend immediately." Bromerys said softly. "He has a mild concussion and needs to be healed quickly. But, I have to ask; what are you doing in a place like this?"

I thought it would take a while to catch Bromerys up to speed on everything that was important, but actually, it was rather quick. I watched the joy on his jovial face vanish and get replaced with malice as I told him that Bethlehem had taken Dawn. It became clear that Bromerys had a soft spot for elves. I felt the natural energy of cheer and fun that radiated from him turn into an overwhelming aura of malevolence.

"Burn this place to the ground, Danyael." Bromerys commanded. It was the first time that I had heard him so serious and grim. "If you cannot end it here tonight, simply call me, and I will help you. Now, I said that I would help your friend, and so I shall. But before I go, I need to see your gun."

I was too terrified to inquire why. I simply handed Bromerys my sawed-off and waited for him to return it to me. He held it aloft in his large hand, like a toy pop-gun held by a giant. His eyes lit up with an emerald fury, dancing with light and energy that I had never seen before. He spoke words in a language that I had never heard before as he held is opposite hand over the weapon.

"It is done." Bromerys announced as he handed me my firearm.

"What is done?" I asked.

"It has the blessing of the hunt on it now." Bromerys announce as he knelt and picked up Rook effortlessly. "Anything fired from that gun will be a sure kill. Anything that falls prey to you while you hunt with that weapon will assure you are victorious. My father channeled the blessing directly into it through me. It's time we remind some of these fools that the Old Gods were feared by humans and fae alike for good reason. Go now, make haste. The blessing only lasts for the day."

A gust of wind scented with grass and elderberries rushed down over us. I flinched in response, only to look up and find Rook and Bromerys gone. I loaded my gun and pulled the door open far enough for me to enter. I stepped into the den of monsters who were once men and prepared myself for what I was about to do. It was a surprisingly easy choice tonight. I walked down the cement hallway and came to another door. This one was not as sturdy as the outer door and was unlocked. It had a bar across its middle section to serve as the door handle. The type you see at school gymnasiums or government buildings.

I took a deep breath and threw the door open with every ounce of strength that I could muster. It flew open with well maintained ease, slamming into the wall as it did a full one-hundred eighty degree rotation. I heard the sounds of inner workings snap and break, but ignored their existence. I had bigger problems.

I found myself looking into a giant amphitheater style open expanse room. Dining tables were set up everywhere, as people dressed in church clothes sat around them. A large circle table was at the opposite end of the room, with a giant cross at its center. Bound to this cross was Dawn.

Blood filled tubes trailed out her body, running into fixtures with taps on them. I felt my rage growing, as the scene set into my mind. I let my fury boil over, as every dark corner of my mind screamed for release. I let them. I let go of every ounce of self control that I had and felt cold rage replace the heated anger that I felt.

"WHAT HAVE YOU DONE TO HER?!" I shouted at the room. Several people pushed themselves in their chairs away from me. They were the only ones who had the right idea. "DAWN, I AM GOING TO GET YOU DOWN FROM THERE, AND THEN I AM GOING TO KILL EVERY LAST ONE OF YOU IN THIS ROOM!"

I reached for Crowley's power again. No, it was my power now. Not Crowley's. He was dead and I remained. I willed the energy that heeded my beckoning to seal all of the doors and it obliged. I stepped through the door and let my powers close it behind me. I could smell the scent of melting steel again as the door welded itself shut. It was then that the rest of the people understood what was going on and panic ensued. I ignored their fear and trepidations and walked straight for Dawn.

I was almost to the table when Zachariah stepped in front of me. His face was controlled, but clearly upset. The cool and collected confidence he had earlier today was gone. All that remained was the frail shell of a putrid man. I expected him to attempt some sort of violence. He didn't. He lifted a wine glass full of Dawn's blood to his mouth and drank it all in one motion. He lowered the glass, revealing a smug smile, thinking he had done something great. He had. I decided that he was the first to die. In a swift motion that I had never displayed before in my life, I pulled my gun and squeezed the trigger.

The dragon's breath rounds had been intense and beautiful before. Now they were otherworldly. The fire was no longer white and blue. It had transformed into a rainbow inferno of various colors. Crimson, vermillion, golden-yellow, emerald, azure, indigo... so many shades of colors danced wildly in that blast of flame that roared out of the barrel of my gun. Yet instead of the usual blast of a forceful inferno, a concentrated stream of conflagration lanced out in a controlled blast straight through Zachariah's forehead. A smoldering hold sizzled directly between his eyebrows before his body dropped beneath its own weight.

Let me correct my statement earlier. It was here that the members of Bethlehem truly understood what was about to happen. Scream erupted among the crowded banquet hall as people flooded to the doors, trying to escape their fates in vain.

I walked to the cross, and looked at Dawn in pain, bound to that wooden monstrosity. I noted a table with a bone saw and a sharp looking carving knife. I grabbed the knife and began severing her restraints. One by one, her appendages came free from their bindings and I felt my own pain welling up in my throat. I dared not remove the tubes for fear that I would do her more harm. I dared not mar her body further.

I couldn't feel her pulse nor could I hear her breathing. Torturous feelings bleed into my rage as the truth of Dawn's fate seized my mind. I turned back to the assorted members of Bethlehem, and let my rage fill me. They all would know suffering before they knew death.

CHAPTER 21
SUCH A WASTE

Dawn awoke to find herself tied firmly to a crucifix with an almost circular table erected around her. The table was massive, one of the largest that she had ever seen before. There was about a four foot gap that cut straight to where she was being held. The area around contained an additional four foot radius between her and the rest of the table. Her heart began to race as panic welled up in her throat.

The last thing that she remembered was looking at her reflection in the face of that mirrored golem and it pushing its face to hers. After that, it was all a blank. She had no recollection of how she arrived at where she was. There was a large banquet hall that spread out around her, sparsely lit and furnished with various tables and chairs, like a diner, only on a grander scale. There were no windows, and the air felt stifled and unmoving. Dawn knew that they were underground.

She saw only three doors. One with a small window slit in it, brightly illuminated and giving a glimpse of what was possibly a kitchen area. There other two were plain, heavy doors obviously designed to be secure.

It was hard fan the flames of her courage when the storms of terror and hopelessness pressed in at her from all sides. Her eyes darted around her frantically searching for some sign of hope that she could cling to. What she found was horror dressed in a business-formal suit.

Elder Zachariah sat comfortably in a chair not fifteen feet from the table, staring at Dawn hungrily. The look in his dead, hungry eyes was the essence of nightmares and dread. She felt tears threaten to run free in the face of her current predicament. And then she heard Danny's voice in her head, and despite the cynicism accompanied behind his words, it was almost a comfort.

"Wait for it; he's doing to do a villain monologue!" Danny's voice said in his typical smug drawl.

And despite the terror, fear, and inevitable doom that had set in her being, Dawn smiled at the thought of his voice. That was definitely something that he would say. In the short time that she had known him, his jaded cynicism had become charming in its own way. Now she faced certain death, she just wanted to see the idiotic nerd one more time.

"I see that you have awakened." Zachariah soothed. "I am so glad. You and I have a… personal matter to discuss with you."

"I would appreciate it if you didn't toy with me." Dawn answered hollowly. "I know what your organization does, I know what you are, and I know what you are going to become."

"Oh, do you now?" Zachariah mocked. "Well that will save me time then. I hate to waste anything, time especially. Now then, since you know what we do, I will tell you the why. We do not eat people. We imbibe their life. We take the remaining time that they have and ingest it so that we may expand our own lives. We do provide the very services our organization publicly advertises, but only because we need to cull the heard. If left unchecked, humans would grow rampantly and continue to waste and destroy. We simply pick off those who waste the most in an area. Think of it like recycling, but with life force."

"Danny, get me a phone because you called it." Dawn laughed to herself. "So what does this have to do with me?"

"Straight to the point I see." Zachariah smiled wickedly. "I love it. You are something that I have never encountered in all of my years. You are clearly fae, but you exhibit none of their weaknesses. You are almost human in my observations, and obviously pass as human to the untrained and ungifted. Not only that, but you are fetching temptation in the flesh. I find myself hungering, but in a new way that none have induced in me before you. It baffles me that I could hunger for something, no someone, as I hunger for life itself. So I make you this one offer. Join me. Take my hand and serve me. You will not want for anything. Serve me, or be served as the main course at tonight's event. Decide quickly, because we are due to start soon, and if I do not remove you from the menu, you will not leave here with your life.

Dawn felt her heart sink. She wanted to live. But she knew that his offer was no offer at all. She would be a prisoner again. She would simply be trading her old jail cell for a collar and a leash. She could try to free him, but something told her that she would never get the chance too. She could wait for him to finish his transformation into a wendigo, but then he might eat her before she escaped. No, there was no option for her currently. But she didn't have to die like a meek and helpless whelp.

Dawn would leave this life with her head held tall and proud. For her parents, for her adopted parents, for Danny, for herself…

"Hey, I don't want to sound ungrateful for such a serial killer level creepy offer, but I am going to have to decline with a gratuitous go fuck yourself!" Dawn replied, as she poised herself with a strength that she thought that she had lost long ago.

"So be it." Zachariah replied. His expression went from excitable to stoic, which made his countenance more sinister that before. "I would like you to know that you will be conscious for this. All of this. You have been giving a pharmaceutical dose of anticoagulants to keep your blood from clotting. You will be drained of your blood, slowly. But not all of it. There will be enough for you to cling to existence. You need to be alive for the transfer of life force to transpire. Those who have paid their dues and have earned their place at the table will drink unto you and take the purest form of your life's essence. Once done, you will be surgically carved and served to the remaining members until you are consumed to a point that the light vanishes from your eyes and you pass."

"You all are a bunch of sick bastards."
Dawn spat. "My comfort is knowing that when
my friend finds this place, and finds all of you,
he will destroy you all."

"Empty threats do not serve you."
Zachariah sighed.

He lifted his hand and gestured at the
kitchen door. Various fae and emaciated humans
came out in serving apparel and began setting
the hall. In a matter of moments, plates, cups,
and silverware had been placed in front of every
chair. And as swiftly as they entered and
completed their work, the multitudes of wait
staff disappeared back into the kitchen.

The whispers of hushed voices began to
trickle through the door directly behind
Zachariah. Soon, the chorus of many footsteps
shuffling followed the sounds of conversation.
And finally, a tide of bodies entered the room.
All were dressed in suits and dresses, clearly
their Sunday Finest. Nothing said church even
like consuming people. As the bodies began
filling the sea of chairs, a set of two humans
exited the kitchen carrying a large silver tray
covered with a pristine white cloth each.

The pair made their way down the split in the table and walked straight to Dawn. It was here that a third human exited the kitchen, this one carrying a small, collapsible table, just large enough to accommodate both trays held by the carrier's peers. The table barer followed the exact path that the other two had, almost as if they had been trained to walk in very specific places only. He set the table up and exited as quickly as the others. The other two set their trays down and lifted the cloths draped over them, revealing the contents of each. A plethora of various surgical tools and serving utensils were carefully placed in precision placement on each tray.

Dawn knew this was it. A part of her desperately hoped that Danny was going to burst through those doors at any moment and save her, but she knew that was a pipe dream. He would be looking for her, sure, but Dawn knew that he was never going to make it in time. The two waiters grabbed a series of tubes and plunger syringes and approached Dawn. She was unable to move, but she was able to control her reactions. She wasn't going to give Zachariah or the rest of them the satisfaction of seeing her cry. She would hold her head high until she could no longer.

There was a pinching sensation in her arm as one of the syringes entered one of her arteries. After a few moments, she had at least 6 tubes running from various parts of her body. She looked out and met Zachariah's smug expression and held firm to it. Locked eyes with him, and felt emptiness. She didn't experience anything like what she was prepared for. All she felt was emptiness and hunger. He was close to turning. She would probably be his last meal before the transformation took place. Then he would turn on the rest of these vile people. He would devour them as they had so many others.

The presence of many individuals filled the seats surrounding the table encircling Dawn as she stared at Zachariah with as much menace as she could manage. She felt the sensation of water trickling over her skin and she started to grow cold. She knew that it had begun and that it was going fast. Her head began to nod as she found her strength fleeing from her. She grew tired and heavy as the sounds around her became dull and muffled. Everything was fuzzy and faded into a fog that began to envelope everything around her. Dawn could faintly hear the noise of something slamming heavily and the noise of multiple chairs scraping against the floor hurriedly. As she faded into blackness, Dawn could almost hear Danny's voice yelling to her. It brought her peace.

CHAPTER 22
LET IT BURN

In the chaos erupting around the room, something happened that I hadn't planned for. Apparently the adrenaline and fear of demise triggered a change in the elders who had gathered at the table around Dawn. Every one of them began transforming into a wendigo as the screams and wailing distracted me.

I was ready to burn this room to cinders when the first roar from the elders grabbed my attention. I had laid Dawn down gently and was in the middle of reloading my sawed-off when I turned to find the gruesome scene of eight bodies contorting on the floor in grotesque and disfiguring positions. This should have terrified me, but something inside me kept me calm. I let the cold lucidity of whatever held my fear and morality at bay, wash over me as I prepared to put the elders of Bethlehem out of their misery.

As I flicked the barrels of my gun closed, the first of the eight stood up. It wasn't quite complete with its transformation, as its ribs and various bones and cartilage snapped into their new positions. The feral and cannibalistic monster that stood before me was designed by magic to be an efficient killing machine.

So, I addressed it with the due respect worthy of its power. I pointed my gun at it and let the fireworks start with. My finger smoothly squeezed the trigger as I stepped close enough for it to touch me. Which, it never got the chance to do so.

"I want you to burn, and then die." I said coolly.

For some reason, the blast from this shell was much different than the one that I had fired to dispatch Zachariah. The colors were the same, but the intensity and size of it seemed to be largely different. It was as if the gun and shell were reacting to my will and firing with an intensity to match the results that I was wanting. The multicolored flames spiraled out in an almost fluid-like fountain of fiery death. It was like a tentacle of liquid lashed out and coiled around the wendigo in front of me, while little drops of incendiary lava rained down on the still forming bodies behind it. Its death was quick, because whatever holy energies had been imbued in the shells and gun itself seemed to be adding to the potency of lethality against the wendigos. It burned to ash in a matter of seconds. The small splashes that had struck against the ones behind had burned fissures straight through, leaving cauterized holes.

I reloaded as quickly as I could, glaring daggers at the rising bodies of the seven remaining wendigos. I focused my wrath on them, letting it feed my speed and adrenaline. I had a whole room to bring down and it was only a matter of time before the welds that held the door buckled under the sheer volume of weight being thrown against them.

"Work, work, work…" I sighed sardonically.

Like before, my will was carried out through the fire before me. I swayed the stream of fire back and forth like a water hose, making sure that I drenched every one of the elders in the embroiled incineration. They burned as quickly as the first, and when all that remained was smoldering cinders of their remains, the only sounds left in the room were the muffled, uncontrollable sobbing from the people trying to escape. It was almost church like. The quiet seeped into me and felt wrong. I felt something should be said; no it needed to be said. It was here in this moment that I decided to speak out for the first time.

"You! All of you consider yourselves holy." I shouted to the room as I reloaded my gun. "You, who have preyed on those less fortunate than you, be they fae or human. You did more than take their lives; you consumed them in a sick concept of gaining the time they had left. And where has that gotten you?! Did you not see what the elders became?! Have you not seen other members turn into those monsters before?! Did you not think that one day, your organization was going to take things too far? Did you think for one second that all of you might bite off more than you could chew? Well I am here tonight to answer those question, whether you asked them or not. You all have been weighed. You all have been measured. And you all have been found wanting. Your sins are greed, pride, and gluttony. And I am here to collect on your dues. I have judged you all guilty. The punishment is death! I will kindly see you all in hell when it is my time, but until then… keep me a spot warm until I arrive!"

I let my mind and emotions drift to the night that I had met Dawn. I let myself feel the same energy that I had then. I remembered what had happened when I used the power that I inherited from Crowley to set the Order's prison ablaze; and then I called it forth to do the same here.

I inserted my dominance, my will into it, making sure that it would not harm Dawn, and then let it out. I told it what I wanted it to do. I made it reach out engulf everything. And then I walked away. I picked Dawn's lifeless form up and made my way to the other door that I hadn't opened. I didn't know where it led, but I was guessing it was where all these people had entered from. I set my power to unseal it long enough for me to pass through. As I did, the sounds of footsteps running behind me alerted me that someone was trying to get out with me. I stopped them. I willed a concussive force of air to release behind me, knocking the would-be escapee back into the banquet hall. As the door swung shut behind me, I sealed it again. I simply kept walking and let the fire of my will burn everything behind me.

I held Dawn close to me as I followed the dimly illuminated walkway, unaware and not caring where it led. It was going to burn as well. Eventually we passed through another set of metal doors and emerged into what I could only describe as an actual church. It was an expansive convention floor. It was all set up for some event yet to take place. And event that would never happen here. The stage and sound equipment were prepped and waiting, as was the army of chairs in straight lines from wall to wall. I ignored it all and just made my way to an exit.

After many more large, high-vaulted ceilings and expansive rooms, I exited the church of Bethlehem into a parking lot unlike any that I have ever seen. The building was nestled on the top of a hill, and I could see open fields for miles around. It didn't matter, it was going to burn. Bethlehem ended here tonight.

"Oh my goodness, well done!" A flamboyant voice called from behind me.

Lucifer stood at the double-door archway of the church with a wicked smile on his face. His hands were in a slow, mocking applaud. Or it may not have been mocking. He was the devil after all.

"Here to collect finally?" I asked bitterly. "I honestly don't really care."

"Oh no." Lucifer laughed gleefully. "You delivered beautifully. Consider our account settled."

"What do you mean?" I asked, horrified and curious all the same.

"You delivered unto me the damn souls of an entire congregation of sinners!" Lucifer admonished. "And your speech was amazing. I love a mortal who intends their puns!"

"Wait?! What?!" I asked.

"Bethlehem was something that has been on the radar of both Heaven and Hell for some time now." Lucifer answered informatively. "But I knew with my Dad's ignorant 'No direct contact' rule, nothing was ever going to get done about them. So, the right whisper here and there to get them close enough to you, a little nudge to your father laced with inspiration to keep you and Rook busy, and voila! Results."

"You set this up?" I shouted.

"Guilty." Lucifer laughed, shrugging his shoulders. His white suit never even creased.

"Dawn died because of you!" I screamed in anger. "She is gone!"

"Yeah, that wasn't by my design." Lucifer replied. It was the first time that he spoke and sounded sincere. "Listen Danny. I mean this when I say it, but I didn't wish your elf ill will. I didn't plan on her dying. In fact, I love the fae because they piss my Dad off so much. We can't bring them back. Our powers don't touch them in death. Surely my baby brother has told you this."

"He has…" I replied as tears began rolling down my face. "I didn't want this. I didn't want to feel anything like this ever again. I liked her damn it. She made me feel like I was worth a damn! And now she's gone. She's gone and I am crying and pouring my heart out to the devil! Life sucks so much!"

"Yes, well, you'd be surprised how often I hear things much like this." Lucifer answered stiffly. "And yes, life does suck. Get up man! You're Danny fucking-Nimbus! Scourge of the fae and monsters that prey on humans. And just so you know, you're not on my list of future guests. At least not yet."

"Even with what I just did?!" I asked as I looked up from embracing Dawn.

"You didn't kill any innocent souls down there." Lucifer laughed. "In fact, I'm not sure that you killed any humans. You did both sides a favor here. These people were past redemption. They wouldn't have recognized divine intervention if the heavenly host showed up."

And like that he was gone. I stood there in that parking lot atop of that hill staring at the church of Bethlehem burning. The flames had grown at this point, creeping out from the crevices of the building, licking and eating everything they could light up. I reached out with my mind and forced the fire to burn until the building and all that was inside was gone. To burn Bethlehem and nothing more.

As the sun began to rise on the horizon, I held Dawn's body close to mine, wishing that she was still alive. I only wanted to see her smile one more time. I looked down at her face, and was surprised to see that very site. A small, remnant of a mischievous smirk remained splayed on her lips. I let myself smile despite the pain and touched my head to hers. I would not repeat the same mistake that I made with Nisa.

"I release you, Dawn." I whispered between tears. "Go now, and find peace."

I gave her body one last embrace, one last hug, and as I did, something unexpected happened. Her body vanished into light, leaving her clothing draped in my arms. It was like something out of Star Wars, as the light drifted away from me, and then faded into the rising sun. I stood there, blinking the tears from my eyes.

I was confused and distraught and had no idea what had just happened. I stood up, looking at her clothes in my arms, the last remains of her existence that I had. I rolled them up, tucked them under my arm, and made my way to find a vehicle to take to get back home. As I turned around, I came face to face with Bromerys this time.

His tall form cast a large shadow over me. I looked up into his face and tried to keep from breaking.

"I was too late." I whispered, holding up her clothes.

"No, boy," Bromerys smiled. "You saved her. She was able to be at peace and move on. Her soul would have never been able to find peace if she had been consumed by those monsters. But you kept that from happening. You stopped them and she was able to move on to the Shores of Light."

"The Shores of what?" I asked.

"The Shores of Life is the afterlife of the elves." Bromerys replied. "Her body turned to light and moved on, right?"

"Yeah." I answered.

"Then know that she is at peace." Bromerys smiled. "Rest easy knowing that you were her hero. Again, Danny, you are a hero."

"No, I am not." I replied, reflecting on my calm acceptance of murdering the members of Bethlehem. "But that's ok. I don't want to be the hero. Heroes have to play by rules. And I am tired of rules. From here on out, I will be doing things my way. Now, I need to see Rook. Can you take me to him?"

"Of course." Bromerys smiled grimly.

The scent of cut grass and honey danced in the air, and then we were traveling. Much the same way that we traveled with Azrael… go figure.

CHAPTER 23
FROM THE ASHES, RISES

Rook and I spent the next several weeks tracking down all of the fae who were connected to Bethlehem. Despite the occasional concerned look, Rook had remained mute about what had happened. The only thing that he had said was the less he knew, the better.

Then there was the fire. Sadly to say, it had not remained as contained as I had hoped. My control over my power was not enough to contend with Mother Nature. Some dry grass by the labyrinth had caught fire and lit an area ablaze out by a highway. Experts ended up casting the blame on chains dragging against the asphalt of the road, or some such nonsense. Human minds were still not ready to address magic being reality.

The only good thing about the raging fire destroying the landscape around Shasta County, was that it flushed many of the fae that we were hunting into the open and made it easier for Rook and I to confront them. Well, easier being a choice word. The trolls that Bethlehem seemed to have indentured to them weren't easy to take down because of their size and strength.

Conversely, fire was one of the trolls' only weaknesses, so they weren't particularly rational with the blazing wildfire destroying everything around them; which made it simpler for us to outsmart and outmaneuver them.

Rook and I had just dispatched one particularly nasty one that had been eating transients under a bridge by the local casino. He had also been going upstream and grabbing employees and patrons at the casino and hotel and leaving a trail of corpses that the local authorities were blaming on a bear. Wildlife experts were baffled by the supposed behavior, blaming the fire for such drastic and misplace actions. Why couldn't they just say they didn't know what killed those people and leave it at that? Why did they feel the need to explain away everything? It didn't make the threat any less real. That was my job.

"Do they have to smell worse than they look?" Rook asked, as he slipped on a face mask in an attempt to filter the smell.

"Sadly, that's pretty mild." I replied. "This one happens to be cleaner than they usually are because it nested next to a water source."

"Ugh… tell me again, why do I help you with this part?" Rook asked as he turned away from the massive troll corpse.

"Because you know that I can't do it all by myself?" I met his glance and arched an eyebrow.

"Keep telling yourself that." Rook chuckled as he made his way up the hill from under the bridge. "Anyways, how many more do you think are left?"

"I'm not sure." I replied, catching up to him. "We have had to deal with so much. I'm shocked that Bethlehem had managed to shang hai so many fae into their service."

"Well, from what that hag told me, you can thank the Order of Saint Patrick for that." Rook huffed as he slowed his pace. "As long as they're trying to kill fae for no reason, there will always be refugees, and refugees will shelter in any port that harbors them safely."

"Yeah… I've been thinking about that myself." I replied, knowingly. "And I have only one conclusion."

"What's that?" Rook asked as we crested the hill onto even ground.

"It's simple. We take down the Order of Saint Patrick." I answered.

"Ha!" Rook barked. "Are you daft? Did that fire burn your brain cells?"

"Nope." I replied. "We can't fight all of them, sure. But if we cut the head off of the snake, the body dies."

"So, how do you propose that we do that?" Rook asked. "That's not exactly an easy feat."

"Well, my dear old dad is the lynch pin in their Order, they just don't know it." I stated malevolently. "He has connections to both you and I, so it shouldn't be hard to use that to our advantages. Once we get Vergil on board, it's just a massive game, like Mouse Trap."

"Don't you mean chess?" Rook asked skeptically.

"No, I mean Mouse Trap." I answered. "This is going to take some preparations and build up. Not to mention, I want pops to see the dominoes falling as the trap is triggered. I want him to see it happening and know that he's helpless."

"You're sounding a bit like a fae there." Rook warned.

"Well, I'm not saying that the fae do things the wrong way." I replied. "It's just a matter of marrying their methods with the right application. Trust me, I have thought about this for a long time now."

"There is one thing that I have learned in my years as in law enforcement," Rook added, "those who say 'Trust me,' typically cannot be trusted."

"Are you saying that I can't be trusted." I asked.

"Maybe I am." Rook answered absently. "Or maybe I am saying that you can't trust yourself anymore. I don't want to see you fall any farther than you already have."

"You're finally catching on to this magic and supernatural crap." I laughed. "Perhaps you're right. Maybe I can't trust myself anymore."

"Holy crap!" Rook gasped. "Someone call the papers, Danyael MacClaude admitted I am right!"

"Shut up and listen for a second." I laughed. "What I am saying is that's why I need your help, now more than ever. I know that I am slipping. I don't give a damn about the things that I did when I first got involved with this life. Knowing that I can use magic now, I cannot trust myself to use it the right way. After Bethlehem, I now know how far I am capable of going given to right or even wrong push. I need you to watch me and promise me one thing."

"Don't get all dire on me kid." Rook warned. "Don't ask me something that I cannot do."

"I still have to ask." I replied. "If I step over that line, if I go too far, will you take me out. Do you have the strength to do the right thing by me? Can you do what is morally right?"

"Damnit Danny!" Rook snapped.

"Will you promise me, Rook?!" I interrupted.

"Only if it comes to that!" Rook answered heatedly. "Only, and I do mean only if I feel that you have gone beyond redemption."

"Thank you." I sighed.

"If Stephen will not, I will." Vergil's voice called from behind us. Rook and I turned aggressively, our instincts gearing us to act fast. "Easy now fellows. Azrael said that I was needed here. He said that now our paths aligned and we would need to work together. Tell me, why would he say such a thing?"

"We're going to take out the Order of Saint Patrick." I announced. "Starting with my bastard of a father!"

"Well then, perhaps I should share the information that I have discovered with you." Vergil answered wearily. "But first, let us adjourn to a more private setting. The wind itself has clever ears and loose tongues these days."

"Agreed." Rook huffed. "I'll drive. You both scare the crap out of me when you drive. Also, we will be stopping to get breakfast. MacClaude and I have been at this all night."

"Very well then, lead on." Vergil smiled, gesturing for Rook to continue walking.

"You guys go on, I'll catch up." I said as I looked towards the east.

Vergil nodded, but Rook lingered and stared at me sternly. I looked up at him a smiled absently.

"Are you ok?" He asked.

"I am fine." I answered, looking back to sunrise.

"Ok, we'll be at the truck." Rook added.

I nodded, giving no attention to if he actually left or not. Something more important had my attention. The sun crested over the tree line in the distant, flashing the radiant orange and red colors over the clouds as it illuminated the smoky sky and drove back the night. The warmth of the rays fell on me, embracing me for just a flash. And in that moment, even though I knew it wasn't real, I felt Dawn in my arms one more time. I smiled, hearing her voice in my head calling me a nerd, as I let the feeling go, and let her move on. I turned around and walked back to where Rook and Vergil was waiting for me. I climbed in the back seat, and waited for Rook to start driving. After a few minutes of quiet, I broke the silence.

"Alright, Vergil." I said. "Tell me what's the fastest way to take my dad and the other heads of the Order out?"